The

Of

Firefighting

Ben Hughes

Note for Librarians: A cataloguing record for this book is available from Library and Archives Canada at www.collectionscanada.ca/amicus/index-e.html
ISBN 1-4120-7171-2

Printed on paper with minimum 30% recycled fibre. Trafford's print shop runs on "green energy" from solar, wind and other environmentally-friendly power sources.

TRAFFORD PUBLISHING™
Offices in Canada, USA, Ireland and UK

This book was published *on-demand* in cooperation with Trafford Publishing. On-demand publishing is a unique process and service of making a book available for retail sale to the public taking advantage of on-demand manufacturing and Internet marketing. On-demand publishing includes promotions, retail sales, manufacturing, order fulfilment, accounting and collecting royalties on behalf of the author.

Book sales for North America and international:
Trafford Publishing, 6E–2333 Government St.,
Victoria, BC V8T 4P4 CANADA
phone 250 383 6864 (toll free 1 888 232 4444)
fax 250 383 6804; email to orders@trafford.com
Book sales in Europe:
Trafford Publishing (UK) Limited, 9 Park End Street, 2nd Floor
Oxford, UK OX1 1HH UNITED KINGDOM
phone 44 (0)1865 722 113 (local rate 0845 230 9601)
facsimile 44 (0)1865 722 868; info.uk@trafford.com
Order online at:
trafford.com/05-2066

10 9 8 7 6 5 4

Dedication

Thank you to my family, friends and the fire departments that have supported me along the way and to Trafford Publishing for all that they have done to make publishing this book a reality.

Last but not least a very special thank you goes to Christine and Janine Bell, without them this book would have never happened.

Table of Contents

Smokin'

Fire Stories

My Life

I awoke to the sun shining and the birds singing just as any perfect morning should be. I opened my window to let the clean ocean breeze brush against my face and the hint of salty fresh air entered my room.

My home was a small three-story house, waterfront to a wonderful sandy beach, perfect for any bachelor. Often times I found it to be way too easy to just gaze into the ocean and forget that I even had to go work.

For breakfast I needed something healthy but quick so I threw some multigrain bread into the toaster, and some eggs, red peppers, cheese and bacon into the frying pan. Minutes later I was eating my omelet with fresh strawberry jam smothered toast. With the grub finished I jumped into the shower then threw on my professionally pressed uniform. I could tell today was going to be a good day. I am a firefighter which, to me, is the best job in the world.

I was always early for each of my shifts at the hall so I was in no rush to get to work, but my sports car seemed to make it look that way. I drive a 911 twin turbo Porsche that looked fast even standing still. The distant rumble of the idle was enough to make a grown man tingle; to rev it would make them giddy.

Off to the fire hall and as I sped along my car hugged the countryside switchbacks like it had been glued to the road.

My cell phone rang…it was my good friend Jen whom I haven't spoken to for awhile. She needed a ride into town and knew I would be by her house shortly. I very much looked forward to this because well, hey, Jen was smokin' hot. Could this day get any better, I thought to myself. I pulled into the driveway…no this can't be happening I thought. She had a friend with her who also was completely gorgeous. I had a beautiful brunette in a pink sundress with legs that just wouldn't quit and beside her, this amazing blonde in a blue sun dress which seemed to fit her every curve perfectly. They seemed to walk in slow motion just like you see on T.V. or in the movies. I was speechless. Jen had never looked this good and her friend…WOW! Jen looked in the car as I tried to pull myself together. Jumping out, I opened the door for her as any gentleman would do.

"This is my friend Chantelle" Jen exclaimed, so now I knew this blonde wasn't just a figment of my imagination.

"If you had called sooner Jen, I would have brought the SUV".

"That's okay; Chantelle can sit on my lap".

I tried to contain my joy at this thought, but to see it…uh…oh yeah, I have to go to work. Back in the driver's seat all I can see out of the corner of my eye is two pairs of long legs followed by sexy high heeled shoes and then I scan up at the bodies all the while smelling the gentle intoxicating aroma of their perfumes combined inside the cockpit of my land-locked rocket ship. Every shift of the six-speed manual transmission now comes with a little leg rubbing. This is all too much for me. I need to pray…"Forgive me father for I'm about to sin"…Ok so praying isn't helping either, until the one thing that could distract any firefighter from anything, smoke.

In the distance there is a large amount of smoke coming from one of the apartment buildings.

"Girls hold on, it's time to drop it a gear and get to the hall."

As we neared the structure where the possible fire may exist, I notice that my fire department is not yet on scene. I slow up to quickly assess the scene and check to see if it's been called in; sirens can be heard off in the distance. I can hear echoes from the building lobby, "My Baby! My Baby!" Judging from the building construction, there's no time to go to the hall. I have to act now! I quickly parked. "Girls wish me luck." I make sure I get a kiss on the cheek from each of them……and why not?

I ran to the frantic mother who was screaming in an uncontrollable fit of fear. I managed to calm her down just enough to find out where her baby was. In broken speech and tears she tells me she lives in apartment 421 and her baby girl, Kylie, was still in her crib. Without hesitation, I ran into the building, headed to the stairwell, and ascended to the fourth floor. I didn't have much time. On my hands and knees I scrambled across the floor. Even though I was as low as I could be, the smoke was strong enough to make me cough fiercely. I followed the wall feeling each door for its number 417, 419, 421. I had made it! I checked the door to make sure it wasn't hot. I could hear the infant's desperate screams on the other side of the door even over the rumble of the fire. I had to act quickly, there wasn't much time. Inside the small, dark, smoky, apartment I quickly found little Kylie's room. The baby girl was in her crib. I gently gathered her into my arms and comforted her as I wrapped her in a blanket and put a wet cloth on her face to protect her from what we were about to endure.

Back on my hands and knees, I was ready to take this child back to safety. I checked the door again for heat. It was considerably warmer than when I had entered. Staying behind the door I carefully peered around to see if my original route was still an option. Things had gotten really bad. The hallway I once traveled looked as if it had been opened to the gates of hell. The end of the corridor was now fully involved in fire and spreading rapidly. I had to find a new route and fast. The flames down the hall had reached the flashover point (that happens when the temperatures become so great the fire immediately consumes everything in its path). Fire was rolling down the hall towards us at an alarming rate. I slammed the door shut and we got as far as we could from the flames.

How can you reassure a child when I was losing hope myself? The fire rumbled down the hallway towards the apartment. The flimsy apartment door was no match for the forces this inferno was producing and pushed it aside like paper, exposing us to our nemesis face to face. Our only escape was through the window and I wasn't about to let this heated beast get the best of us. I cradled little Kylie in my arms and jumped, back first, through the window. Everything slowed down, the broken glass twinkled in the sunlight as it fell all around me. The fire bit at my feet as if it were trying to pull me back into the building, little Kylie was silent. The wind in my ears was the only sound I could hear.

The fire hadn't got me, but the four-story fall from the burning building might. I knew the infant I cradled was going to be okay and all I could do was watch as the fire started to devour the exterior of the building before I slammed into the grass at the side of the apartment.

I had heard that your hearing was the last thing to go before you die. Was this it? Sounds from everywhere started to enter my head once again. Kylie began to cry and this was music to my ears. Through my blurred vision I was able to see her reunited with her mother. It was so beautiful to see the love that only a mother can have for her child.

I began to hear some sweet familiar voices. Were they angels I wondered...no it was Jen and Chantelle comforting me. Then the sound of the sirens rang in my ears as I heard the fire engines closing in. My boys would soon be here, I said to myself. I closed my eyes and everything faded into darkness, a slumber which I wondered if I would ever awaken from. All I had left from the outside world was the approaching sirens getting closer and closer only they didn't sound quite right they sounded more like that of a buzzing noise???

The fire engines now felt like they had parked next to my ears. Buzzzzzzzzzzzz what the???...It's my alarm clock!!! I'm late for work....again!!! I jumped from my bed, got dressed and ran for the door, jumped into my old truck and raced to the job site, receiving angry looks and rude gestures from the other motorists along the way.

I'm an electrician by day; I have lots of fun. I often grab other electricians and make zapping noises while they are working on electrical circuits for some very funny reactions! As I drove to work I could still remember my dream. Yes I am a firefighter, but for a volunteer fire department, which means that I need to have a regular, full time job to support me. People often comment on what a good combination a firefighter/electrician is because I can put out any electrical fire I might start. Funny guys. Ha Ha!

Introduction

The experiences of a firefighter can be life changing, sad, exciting, exhausting, frightening and sometimes even funny. I have written down the calls and firefighting stories that I have found to be humourous and memorable. These accounts are based on real life occurrences that have happened to me and some have been passed down from other firefighters that I have met along the way.

And On His Farm He Had...

In our rural community we often get called out to many minor incidents simply because people don't know who else to call for assistance. One day we were called out to a farm because the farmer's sheep had been spooked by a few of the local dogs and were now swimming in the ocean - who knew sheep could swim. Needless to say, our department was in no way equipped for the marine rescue of the farmer's flock so we stood and watched the sheep swim around in the cool ocean waters. All the while the farmer was wondering when we would stick on our super capes so that we could swoop out over the ocean to save the day. The sheep did eventually swim back to shore.

Oh Crap!!!

On this particular day our rural volunteer department was called out to a fire. Everyone was in a panic as it was a rare occurrence for us to be summoned to a real live fire! We all thought - Was this the "BIG ONE" we had all been waiting for?

When we arrived on scene to the code three fire what we found was quite surprising; a smoldering manure pile. The manure had self-combusted and we actually had to put this blaze out! You can only imagine the sight of several proud and dedicated volunteer firefighters who had been waiting to put their much practiced skills of extinguishing a fire to use, knee deep in crap checking for fire extensions. Well what can I say except that call was stinking hot!!!

Deer Firefighters...

This next story is a rescue story with a happy ending. The department was called out to a local home in the district and we were presented with quite an interesting quandary, which would test our problem solving skills. You see, the homeowners had a deer in their swimming pool and after several failed attempts to lasso the deer, one of the firefighters opted to sacrifice his nice warm, dry clothes and jumped in for the rescue. He managed to corral the deer which allowed the other firefighters to get their ropes around the frightened animal; they were then able to pull the beast out of the pool. Needless to say after all that hard work we sure did work up an appetite and ate very well that night - venison was on the menu! Of course I'm kidding about that and after we hoisted the deer out of the chlorinated water, it stumbled around a bit but none the less, very elated to have its hooves back on dry land.

Okay, So Don't Back the Truck Up...

I will start this story off by saying that it isn't meant to be sexist in any manner nor is it to be seen in a stereotypical sense of how women perform on a department. This story is, however, about one woman's behaviour.

One of our new recruits on the department was participating in a driver training session. She was doing very well holding her own with her male peers and was gaining quite a bit of confidence in her driving skills as she kept one of our large pumpers between the lines on the road. In fact, on the whole that day, the driver training lessons were going smoothly.

As this recruit's lesson was coming to an end, her instructor asked her to return to the hall. Slowly maneuvering into a good position, she shifted the truck into reverse and let her foot off the brake, easing it in a backward motion. All of a sudden, a loud BANG, CRASH was heard through the hall as she drove directly through the bay doors, shattering them on impact. She had failed to open the doors!

Fortunately the damage wasn't too extensive, but, as with all embarrassing moments, she will never live it down. As you can imagine, the men at our hall continue to make 'female driver' jabs whenever they have the chance.

That year, this firefighter won our "broken driveshaft" award. This is an award given to the firefighter who makes the biggest mishap that year. And her experience won hands down (or should I say doors down...)

Teepee Terror

There is a native reserve nestled in our quiet, countryside district. Early one evening we were dispatched to the reserve - the call was for medical aid with no other details given. Dusk was just settling in and, as you know, rural areas grow very dark at this time, so we all turned on our flashlights and proceeded to their longhouse, practically feeling our way through the night along the sketchy path.

This night, the natives were having a ceremonial gathering, not an uncommon affair. As we entered the building nothing could have prepared us for what we were about to see. Walking cautiously to the front door, we were greeted by several distressed natives whose faces were black as night. It looked as if we had a brawl on our hands and could only imagine the condition of some of the other people inside the longhouse. We all had the same thought - was it safe for us to enter the building?

As we went through the entrance into the lighted longhouse, our apprehensions were put aside. One of the elders was experiencing chest pains and everyone else had black ceremonial paint on their faces! I guess that's the price you pay for jumping to conclusions.

New Equipment

Some of the hazards when fighting a structure fire are the intense heat produced by the searing flames and the scorching toxic gases given off by the burning building. The simple action of opening a door, allowing cool air to suddenly rush in, can cause an instantaneous explosion to a smoldering fire in a tightly sealed building that is starved of oxygen. This is known as a backdraft.

To prevent a backdraft you have to ventilate the area. To create proper ventilation, you must make an opening in the roof of the structure or break an upper window. This allows the heat and gases to escape without reintroducing large amounts of oxygen.

On this response to a local structure fire, the chief called for ventilation. Wanting instant results, he picked up the nearest garden gnome and tossed it through one of the upper windows. It proved to be a very effective means of fulfilling our ventilation needs, however, after much consideration, we decided against carrying ventilation gnomes on our trucks.

John Deer

It is very typical for volunteer firefighters and career firefighters to attend courses from time to time to brush up on their skills and acquire new ones. Following suit, our department decided to send a select few of our men to a course called "Live Fire". This is a course with the specific goal of training for fighting structural fires. It is a great course that gives firemen the chance to experience a live burn inside a building in a safe and controlled manner.

As they drove back to our hall from the successful and worthwhile training weekend, the driver of one of our vehicles struck a deer! With the wheels locked the truck went spinning uncontrollably down the highway narrowly missing a semi tractor trailer truck. Thankfully the crew, although shaken, were uninjured. However, the irony of the situation is that when the deer flew through the air after impact with our truck, it landed over thirty feet away and came to rest in front of the John Deere™ Tractor supplies dealer.

Nice Truck!!!

A new recruit from a career department wanted to show some of his friends the new equipment he had just learned how to use at his hall. He invited a group of his friends to the hall for a tour and to show off all the apparatus. He decided that it would be a good idea to highlight the ladder truck and show them how it worked. Once he had pulled the vehicle out into the parking lot he proceeded to raise the long ladder, which was capable of reaching heights of 100 plus feet. When the ladder is fully extended, it puts a lot of weight on the truck. Unfortunately, the recruit didn't extend the support feet and started to raise the ladder at an improper angle.

You can probably guess what happened next. The large truck with the ladder extended slowly started to tip over. Nothing could be done at this point to prevent the truck and ladder from smashing down in the parking lot. It landed on guess whose vehicle - the new recruit's brand new truck.

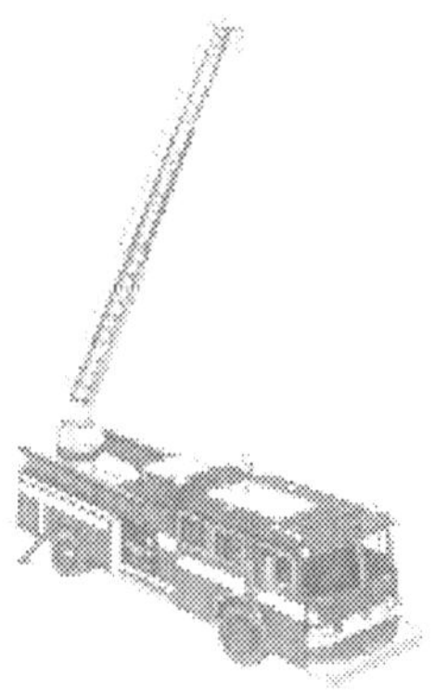

Filler' Up

Volunteer firemen don't necessarily work specific shifts; they go about their day as normal and when dispatched to a call leave what they are doing at the time to respond. On this particular response we all arrived on the scene of a local marina. The tone out described the incident as a boat with a fuel leak so we were there just in case of a fire. The firefighters were directed to the refueling docks where a 30 foot boat was moored.

We approached the owner and began to question him as to what had happened. The owner was just a tad tipsy, appearing to have had one too many beers. Apparently he had simply missed the fuel tank filler hole when he tried to fill up his tank and didn't notice until the boat's hull was completely full of gasoline. The level sloshing around the boat was well above his ankles. The amateur sailor's response to the whole situation was "I thought it was takin' a little more than usual."

Now that the scene had been assessed we had a few options as to how we would deal with the incident. It was too small for the spill agency to deal with so we were fully responsible for the resolution. After hearing some suggestions, our favorite was to push the boat out into the harbor and light it on fire. The chief wouldn't go for this one, so we all took turns bailing, spending much of the day on this task. We all regret not burning it!

I'll Park It Here!!!

The firefighters on this scene were relieved when they found an elderly man in the ditch with his scooter overturned to be ok. Many times when an elderly person has an accident like this it is because they have just experienced a heart attack or stroke or other similar trauma, and being fragile, they often break bones which can lead to spending the rest of their life in a hospital under supervised care.

Responding to this call, the elderly man seemed quite alright and asked for the firefighters' assistance in getting his "ride" upright so he could continue on his way. The firefighters gave him a quick once over and despite the strong smell of booze, the gentleman seemed in good health, so they lifted his scooter out of the ditch and sent him on his way.

The firefighters were all in good spirits as they watched the man drive away. Their mood soon changed, as the old man who was only about a block away, drove his scooter into another ditch, upturning it once again. The blood alcohol content of the senior had definitely taken over his perception skills messing up his judgment. Again the firemen lifted the scooter out of its new found parking spot but this time, despite his pleas, he was not allowed to drive his scooter home.

Head Count

For all structure fires, special personal protection gear must be worn in order to protect the firefighters as much as possible. One of those protection devices is called a Self Contained Breathing Apparatus (SCBA), which protects the firefighter from breathing in hot gasses and toxic fumes while on scene. Attached to the SCBA is a device called a pass alarm. The pass alarm is motion activated. It has a flashing light and audible alarm so if a firefighter has fallen inside a building and ceases to move, the lights start to flash and a very loud alarm sounds.

On one structure fire, an extra SCBA and activated pass alarm that was not in use was left beside our mainline pumper. The unoccupied pass alarm began to sound making it difficult for the pump operator to hear commands over his radio. The pump operator had had enough so he removed the pass alarm from the air pack and tossed it as far as he could into the nearby bushes. Once the pass alarm had stopped bouncing through the bushes it continued to do its job, sending an earsplitting BEEEEEEEEEEEP into the air.

The firefighters continued to fight the fire until someone heard the alarm in the bushes. Not knowing the pump operator had thrown the pass alarm into the shrubbery, the Chief was forced to use some of his manpower to conduct a search of the forest for a potential 'man down' incident. The Chief did the right thing but boy was he mad to find the tossed away alarm.

See Food

Readers must be forewarned that this story is not for someone with a weak stomach. On course for training in live burn situations, one of the trainees was suiting up to go into the burning building. In his anxious state (his first live burn experience) he threw on his air-pack and facemask. As the trainee pulled his mask over his face, he pulled the straps to tighten it as he had practiced many times before. The only difference was that this day, the straps were a little tangled and one pulled against his throat in such a way that it hit his gag reflex. The trainee threw up inside his mask which was now firmly strapped to his head containing most of the vomit against his face. Everyone kept an eye on their masks to make sure they were still using their own the next day.

Glad to Help

A Fire Department in the U.K. received a non-emergency call from an elderly lady whose cat was stuck in a tree (the stereotypical rescue scenario for a fireman). Having a bit of spare time on their hands, the men didn't want to tarnish their golden public image, so the department and its men obliged.

Once on scene, they observed that sure enough the cat was stuck high in the tree. The firefighters quickly went about setting up their ladders and extracting the distraught kitty from the tree. The elderly woman was so ecstatic that her feline companion was now safe on the ground that she invited all the firemen into her home for tea and crumpets. After the men had their fill they thought that it would be best to be on their way, and with cheerful farewells the crew re-boarded their fire engine and backed down her driveway. Much to everyone's horror they had run over the elderly woman's cat, who had decided to take an afternoon bask in her driveway.

Blondes Have All the Fun

On a hot summer's day, the fire department was the first on scene for a drive-by shooting that had been called in by the victim. Once they were sure the scene was safe, they approached the victim who had been shot in the back of the head while sitting in her vehicle. The victim was a lady who appeared to be frantic but alert to the situation, holding the back of her head.

The firemen were not able to observe any broken glass or projectile holes anywhere on the outside of her car, nor could they see any blood, so they asked the shooting victim to remove her hands from the back of her head, but she wouldn't follow their instructions and stated that she was "holding her brain in". After reassuring her that it would be okay to let go, she finally did. The firemen were surprised to find white gooey stuff stuck in her hair. On the back seat of her car were her groceries and the men found one bag containing a croissant tube that had exploded with the heat and shot some of its pastry cream out hitting the lady in the head. Hearing the loud explosion and then getting hit in the head sent her into a panic. Guess what? She was Blonde!

Just Look Harder!!!

A fire officer was training a new female recruit on one of their older water tanker trucks. The recruit really needed practice with the double clutch gear shift this truck had. Most fire trucks are automatics but this one, being just a little bit older, was a standard. The recruit was doing well getting the feel of the motion of shifting the truck in and out of the proper gears. The officer felt it was better to quit while they were ahead so he asked the recruit to drive the truck back to the fire hall.

Now secure in the fire hall, the officer who was so impressed with the recruit's driving skills excitedly asked her if she wanted to see the engine. Not wanting to disappoint her superior, the recruit agreed. The officer pointed to a six inch tube at the rear of the truck in which the engine could be viewed. With the recruit staring into the six-inch tube, the officer taught the recruit that the tube was actually a quick water discharge valve that was capable of releasing 1500 gallons of water in mere minutes, the hard way.

Duck, Duck, Duck....Goose!!!

This rural community was having one of its largest bush fires in years, covering many hectares. Two of the world's largest water bombers, the Martin Mars bombers, were dispatched along with water dropping helicopters to help fight the blaze. The burning was so intense and out of control that the individual department could not handle the scene and sought the aide of four neighbouring departments and numerous plain clothed civilians willing to help to do what they could.

It was several weeks before the fire was fully extinguished and many hot spots would flare up daily under the intense summer heat and arid conditions. The cause of the fire, which has not yet been proven otherwise, was a goose who had flown into a power line which then shorted itself out and fell in the barren grass below, igniting it instantly.

As far fetched as this story may seem the cause has been confirmed in a bush fire of similar proportions set by a squirrel.

MARTIN MARS QUICK FACTS:

*The Martin Mars is the world's largest flying boat ever flown operationally
*There are only two left in the whole world
*Holds 72,000 gallons/27,276 litres of water
*1 drop covers 4 acres (1.6 hectares)
*Picks water up from lakes in about 25 seconds
*Can make up to 37 consecutive drops over a fire
*Runs off of 4 Wright Cyclone engines at 2500hp (1865kw) each
*Wing Span: 200' (61 m)
*Payload: 60,000 lb (27, 216 kg)
*Length: 120 ft (36 m)
*Height: 48 ft (14.63 m)
*Cruising Speed: 190 mph (305 km/h)
*Fuel Consumption: 780 gallons per hour
*Flying Time: 5.9 hours

ACHOO!!!

Our fire department was called out for medical aid assistance in a local prison. Since all the ambulances were tied up, we were first on scene and had to take care of the patient until they arrived. One of our firefighters had bad allergies and that particular day the weather was windy and dry, perfect for spreading pollen and all of the other annoyances that can trigger violent sneezing allergy attacks.

As we assessed the scene and dealt with the patient who was complaining of chest pains, our sneezing and wheezing firefighter had to excuse himself from helping with the patient as he could no longer bear his allergies. The firefighter went outside and blew his nose for all it was worth and waited for his partners to finish securing the patient.

When his comrades exited the prison they informed the sneeze machine that the patient had Hepatitis C. The fireman then realized that he still had the gloves on he was wearing when touching the patient and had blown his nose with them on. Even though it is nearly impossible to transmit Hep C this way, the fireman went into a state of paranoia, running to the first aid kit located on their truck he grabbed the container of disinfectant gel and coated his entire head with a nice thick, gooey, glistening layer.

That's a Bad Spot

Parking can often be difficult, especially in big, busy urban cities. Now be honest, you know how tempting those reserved 'No Parking' zones in front of fire hydrants become when struggling to find a spot that isn't blocks and blocks from your destination.

On this occasion the owner of a brand new BMW felt that he was 'special' enough that he didn't need to find a parking spot other than the very conveniently located, clearly marked "NO PARKING" spot in front of a fire hydrant which was in an ideal location to the shops he was planning on visiting.

As the oblivious driver shopped, the local fire department was called out to a fire in a building located adjacent to the hydrant where the BMW driver had parked.

Usually the driver would receive a parking ticket and the car would be towed if it was parked next to a hydrant. However, on this occasion the department responding to the emergency call had no time to wait for a tow truck. As the car was parked directly in their path of action, the responding crew felt that there was nothing else that could be done but smash through the car windows so they to could run their high-volume supply line through the car to the hydrant. Now the BMW was stuck for many hours until the scene was secure.

On a separate occasion, another not so observant civilian driver was making a quick stop and parked right in front of the fire hall's bay doors. Any aware person would stop and think "...Hmm, I'm at a fire hall and a call could be sent in at any time which means that the trucks will have to leave ASAP. Maybe I shouldn't park in the wide open area in front of the bay doors..."

Of course, while the citizen was wherever they were, there was a tone out and the responding fire crew sprang into action. As they opened the bay doors and saw the car in their path they had no choice but to run over the violator's car with their much bigger fire truck.

In case you're wondering who is responsible for the damage that is caused in an incident such as this, it is at the owner's expense and he not only has to pay for all the damages but also receives hefty parking violation fines.

Excuse Me Firefighter Coming Through!!!

On volunteer departments there is a higher turn over rate of fire fighters. This particular time we ended up hiring a recruit who let's just say was not all there; he was one spark short of starting fire.

For some time our hall wasn't aware of his behavior outside of our presence. As it turns out this recruit had bought his own "Turn-Out" gear (the gear we wear when responding to structure fires) and he would walk around in neighbouring districts that were not in our jurisdiction and try to assist career departments on scenes. He even went as far as to go into buildings and try to enforce fire codes upon the owners.

It was very evident that he was a phony. Not being the slightest bit qualified, he hadn't even finished our basic training course that we give recruits. Word finally reached our department and our chief had no choice but to dismiss him from service. After the incident we continued to hear about him still getting caught in his firefighting gear, trying to be something he was not. Someone should tell him his gear was only good for a Halloween costume.

Oops Wrong Guy!!!

Tough times can happen in any family. This story is about a wife who had had enough of her husband and had made up her mind that it would be best for everyone involved if the two separated.

While the woman and kids were out one day, the husband felt that this would be a good time to visit his old abode to reclaim some of his possessions. When he arrived at the house a sudden burst of anger and frustration toward his wife took over his mind and actions. Without hesitation he lit the house on fire. The man then called 911 and reported his transgression to the police. He told them that he had had the house rigged with explosives and was in possession of a gun and that he was suicidal.

As we arrived on scene the fire was escalating at a very fast rate but due to the nature of the call, (a potential suicide with bombs and a gun) our firefighting efforts were hampered. We were not able to assess the burning building until it was deemed safe by the police.

The house was fully engulfed in flames when we were finally given the okay to fight the blaze. As we entered and began our work, the husband was nowhere in sight. We quickly tamed the inferno enough so that there were only a few small fires left to deal with. All of a sudden one of our men came upon a pink form that had been charred by the fire. He was so disturbed by his gruesome discovery of the husband's body that he fled immediately and refused to re-enter.

After we had finished putting out the fire a new team of rescuers entered the scene to retrieve the charred and burnt body. As they closed in on the form, expecting to see the worst, they discovered that it was actually a large piece of pink insulation that had fallen from the ceiling during the fire.

What had happened to the husband? He was later found by the police, lying in his shed, trying to asphyxiate on propane gas. Instead of waiting for the bomb squad, the police officer yelled at the man who sat up realizing he was still alive and went peacefully with the officer.

The traumatized firefighter is going to be ok but we don't think he will ever be much of an insulator.

You Didn't Like Those...Did You?

We responded to a chimney fire which, if you are not familiar with, occurs when a chimney is not cleaned on a regular basis and a layer of tar-like coating builds up and when it gets hot enough ignites the whole innards of the chimney. If left un-checked a chimney fire can get destroy the entire chimney insert and possibly cause the rest of the house to catch on fire.

There is a special tool that is used to extinguish a chimney fire - a chimney snuffer. The instrument is dropped down into the chimney cavity and then a fine mist is emitted. This mist acts to eliminate as much water damage as possible, that could be caused by a hose if it were sent down the hole.

When working inside the homes of others, we are always mindful of causing any undo damage and when a chimney snuffer is used we rarely even leave a puddle on the floor of the fireplace.

A crew responding to a chimney fire sends two men into the house to check for flame extensions or fire spread beyond the chimney and to see if the fire in the fireplace has been put out. The firefighters carefully cleaned their boots so to not mark up our homeowner's carpets with their sooty treads. Our men followed the procedures to a tee and carefully walked through the house when one of the crewmembers, who is quite a large man, caught his boot under the rug. This caused him to lunge out and as he fell forward he reached out and grabbed the china cabinet to help get his balance again. All of his weight was put onto one corner of the antique furnishing and the cabinet came toppling over. Not only did all of the fine china shatter into a multitude of pieces but the cabinet was broken as well. Needless to say the fireman felt extremely bad about his slip up. We think twice before sending him into buildings now. Some of us even think twice before inviting him over to our own homes.

Yep They Work

Our district has a Department of National Defense training center located within its boundaries and many parts of the facility are used for shooting practice, grenade launching and other firearm practices. The facility also has a cadet camp, which we are often asked to help with - we run fire/emergency drills with the group.

The drills that we run consist of setting off the fire alarm system within the facility to test the speed of the cadet's reaction time. On one occasion when we set off the alarm, the new cadets ran quickly through the corridors of the building to reach and report to their outside safety stations. The exercise went really well and the reaction time of the cadets was superb. It seemed as though everything had gone off without a hitch until we tried to turn the alarm off. Apparently, the electrical room had been re-keyed and no one in the entire DND facility had the new key. Unable to locate a key we decided that it would be best for us to return to our fire hall.

The crew at the DND eventually located a key to the locked room and managed to turn the obnoxiously loud alarm off...several hours later!

New Hairdo

They say that fire safety begins at home, but I guess that this firefighter took his occupation for granted and failed to inform his two daughters of the importance of fire prevention and safety.

It was midwinter when this incident occurred and like many people, this fireman had a wood-burning stove that he used regularly to heat his home during the colder months. It was common practice for the family to throw any burnable paper products into the stove for kindling. Early one morning the fireman went down to start the fire for the day. Before adding the wood he lit the kindling and paper materials that were in the stove to get the fire started.

After throwing in a match the fireman went to the kitchen to start some coffee, leaving the stove unattended. When he returned to add some wood to the small fire he opened the doors and as he did so the fire exploded leaving him temporarily deaf and both his eyebrows and hair singed by the flames. Apparently, when his daughters were tidying their bathroom they disposed of their hairspray cans into the burnable waste bag, not realizing they were highly explosive.

The fireman was more or less okay and made a point of teaching his girls and wife FIRMLY the importance of fire safety at every chance he got while his eyebrows and hair grew back in.

Good Luck

A first grade pet became a local hero when the classroom that it was kept in caught fire. For some reason the fire didn't trip the fire alarm or spread too much and because the fire started in the evening, after the night janitor had left, no one was around to place the emergency call.

As the fire grew larger and engulfed the classroom the flames neared the aquarium that was home to the students' pet. As the flames danced on the glass of the aquarium the little hero sprang into action. Even though the hero was only a goldfish, when the flames hit the glass of its tank the glass grew so hot that it shattered causing the water to rush out onto the fire and extinguished it.

The next morning, when the scene was discovered, the fire department was called in to investigate and found the pint-sized golden hero still alive and well in a puddle of water on the ground. Just goes to show you that heroes come in all shapes and sizes.

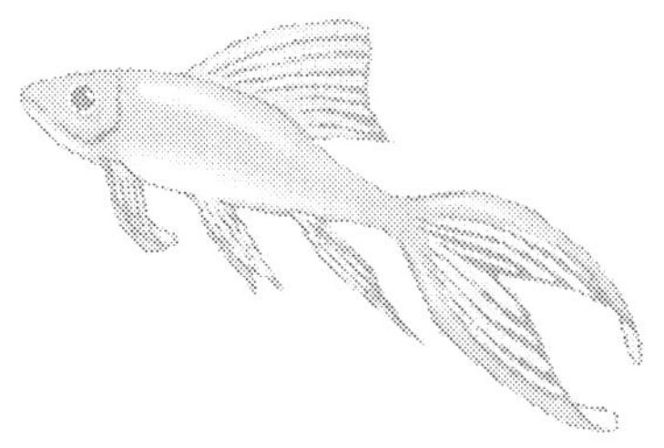

Bad Luck

It was perfect day for a BBQ. There was a calm evening breeze that cooled the hot summer's air and who could resist the opportunity to cook over the open flames of the grill. The family in this story felt that they had to take advantage of the night and opted to grill the salmon that the husband had caught on his fishing excursion, earlier that day.

All prepped and ready to sear, the salmon was gently placed on the grill. The husband then went inside to grab a cold beer from his fridge as the salmon had to cook for a bit before it could be turned over. Unknown to the amateur chef there was a neighborhood raccoon lurking in the bushes just waiting to pounce on the unattended delicacy. The raccoon just couldn't resist the scent of the cooking salmon and at the first chance it jumped onto the BBQ to try to snatch the fish.

Now, as soon as the raccoon jumped onto the hot BBQ he rebounded immediately having burned his little paws. With his abrupt actions, the grill tipped over spraying hot salmon oil all over the side of the house. Before the family had discovered what had happened the tipped BBQ and oils had ignited and the exterior of their house was now on fire. The fire department was called but hundreds of thousands of dollars in damage had already been done by the time they had arrived.

More Good Luck

The "do-it-yourselfer" in the next story took great pride in his work and was so proud being able to install a fireplace in his living room. He had been working for quite some time on his home, renovating it from top to bottom, all by himself.

The homeowner lit the new fireplace in the early morning hoping to warm the house for when he returned home from work. As this was the first time the man had let the fireplace run for an extended period of time, he discovered that the installation had been done incorrectly and while the house was vacant, a fire started and proceeded to spread through the whole room! The flames grew so hot that they burnt through the ceiling, exposing the plastic plumbing lines the homeowner had also installed. Thank goodness for plastic pipes because the flames melted them allowing the water to spray out and extinguish the blaze. When the man returned home he found extensive water damage to his home but hey, that's much easier to mop up and repair than a burnt down house.

And The Bad Luck Continues

The family in this story made the lifetime trip to the "happiest place on earth" - Disneyland! They had thoroughly enjoyed their much needed vacation. As they returned home and pulled into their driveway all appeared just as it was left. They unloaded their luggage from the car and walked casually up their quaint front steps unprepared for what they were about to find when they opened the front door. As they crossed the threshold the family discovered that their entire house had been gutted by fire and had burnt itself out. Not a situation you would be expecting to deal with upon returning from holidays.

When the fire investigators were done their assessment of the scene, they concluded that the cause was an electrical fire from an appliance that had been left on. The reason why the neighbours hadn't realized what was going on inside the home was that the smoke was so thick it blackened out the windows, and because it was a newer home it was virtually air tight and the fire ran out of oxygen and smothered itself before penetrating the exterior walls and roof. I think I can safely say this ruined their vacation.

Neat...Can I Try That Again?

So you think that those little hand-held sparklers you give your kids on occasions such as Canada Day and the Fourth of July are relatively safe, right? WRONG!!! They have been the source and cause of many minor burns and accidents.

On an evening in early May, a young boy was left out in his front yard by his parents to play with his lit sparkler. As the tyke swung the sparkler from side to side leaving glowing lines in the night sky he quickly grew tired of this action and wanted to 'spark' things up just a bit so he took to throwing the sparkler up in the air. What goes up must come down...or does it?

With one toss, the sparkler got stuck in a very large and dry pine tree in the family's front yard. You can probably see where this is going. The tree caught fire and became fully involved. The parents of the young boy raced out of the house when they realized what their son had started. The father ran to grab the hose to try to extinguish the fire himself while they awaited the professionals. What a sight - the family standing in the middle of the lawn, the father shooting a stream from the garden hose up in the air, the mother standing in shock with her jaw agape and the young boy gleaming with amazement at what he had caused.

When the fire department arrived they quickly took action and tamed the blaze. Boy was this family lucky that it was just their tree that caught fire. If the wind had been blowing in the other direction, a few sparks could have easily wafted to their house and that would have been quite the fireworks display!

Open Sesame

When at the scene of an emergency a firefighter can often get tunnel vision. Tunnel vision occurs when adrenaline and focus take over your mind and actions and makes it very difficult to see the bigger picture.

Arriving at an emergency can be a bit nerve racking as you never know what to expect. On one occasion two firefighters were commissioned by their captain to gain access into a house that was on fire through the garage door. Quickly they sprang into action and were firmly determined to over take their formidable opponent - the door. They tried prying it open with several different tools expelling all of their efforts and strength into this task. Nothing was working and the men were growing quite frustrated when suddenly the door magically opened. The captain was inside the garage waving at his men to enter.

What had happened was the team of two men had gotten tunnel vision. They were so dead set on entering the garage through the main door that they failed to see the side door that was unlocked - an easy in. Similar instances have happened in motor vehicle accidents where someone forgets trying alternative means at rescuing trapped patrons, instead they jump ten feet ahead and attempt to pry them out through jammed doors. The simple lesson here: Try before you pry!

DUDE Where's My Car?

Our rural fire department was called out to a motor vehicle accident, an all too frequent happening on our winding, twisty country roads. Laying in someone's front yard was a car quite banged up - not the lawn ornament they had been hoping for. The strange thing was that the driver was nowhere to found.

The scene was an absolute mess. There was trash everywhere and we did our best to tidy up before the police arrived by documenting and tossing all the empty beer cans into the abandoned vehicle so that they could conduct a proper investigation.

A young man arrived on the scene by foot. His face was all banged up, his clothes and general appearance were in disarray and he appeared to be quite intoxicated. The young man had been looking for his "stolen" car. He made a point of speaking with the police officers, trying really hard not to slur his words, telling them that his car had gone missing at some point during the night.

As we tended to his cuts and scrapes, making sure that he was okay, one of the police officers questioned him about the happenings of the night and the tipsy patron explained that a car thief had fought him for his car keys and that's why he was so banged up. Being in the middle of nowhere the officer had a hard time believing the story but listened intently to the account. The young man then sealed his own fate when he accidentally pulled a set of car keys out of his pocket. The policeman asked the man if he could use the keys as a source of evidence against the 'would-be' thief.

The 'would-be' thief was none other than the car owner himself. It seems what had happened was that the intoxicated, young man was driving out to the country and drove off the side of the road crashing into the yard, hence the reason for all the trash and beer cans. He then stumbled away and hid while waiting for the police to arrive to try out his story. He figured not only could he get away with being drunk but also have insurance cover his car repairs. He was very wrong.

This would be another reason not to drink and drive.

I'm Here!!! I'm Here!!! Don't Leave Without Me!!!

In a volunteer fire department the firefighters are given pagers and when an accident or fire, etc. occurs the crew are called out to the incident. This allows them to have their own lives, and if the tone on their pager goes off, the volunteer firefighter responds to the hall as quickly and safely as possible. Career departments run a little differently. The career hall is manned 24 hours a day by a paid crew (usually a day shift and evening) so there is always a staff available to respond immediately to an emergency.

The problem with the volunteer hall system is that the firemen get so excited when they have the opportunity to respond to a call and there is such a large group that it almost becomes a race to see who can jump into the fire trucks first to attend a scene. Nobody wants to be left behind.

Some of the responding men get so worked up and their adrenaline starts pumping that when the responders are arriving at the hall, driving so fast, that when they pull up to park on the gravel road side, they skid and hit the other parked cars belonging to their peers. One time, one young firefighter hit the grass and ran right into a tree. We sure gave him a hard time about that.

Other times there have been instances where the responding men forget to turn off their vehicles and when they return from the call, they have run out of gas. There has even been an account of certain volunteers who forget to put their cars in park. They just jump out of their vehicle. When this happens, after the crew returns to the hall, they have a whole new rescue scene that has to be dealt with, as cars have to be pulled out of ditches. I guess fire isn't the only hazard of the job on a volunteer department.

And response isn't the only thing that differs from volunteer to career departments. On a career hall every member of the force has matching uniforms that must be worn at all times. On a volunteer hall things are a little different as there are no uniforms that the crew has to wear. When calls come in the responding firefighters are called in from outside the hall and have to put what they were doing on hold. This means for some interesting sights and laughs. You can see everything from responders in business suits to beach gear, suds still in hair from interrupted showers; pajamas to yard clean-up or mechanic coveralls. One time a volunteer even responded in a Hallowe'en costume.

Regardless of the difference in procedures between the two types of halls, the personnel and their devotion to helping others is still the same and both should be thanked for the hours and efforts they devote to the lives of others.

Chief on Ice

It was an icy, winter day and despite radio warnings, many drivers still chose to drive faster than they should have considering the slippery road conditions. All the volunteer men at our hall knew that there would be an increase in the number of callouts that day. As the calls came in, we decided that the best vehicle in which to respond was one of the larger fire trucks, as it was heavy and would provide good traction on the treacherous roads. The driver still drove carefully and cautiously just to be on the safe side.

Upon arrival to yet another scene that day, we were all starting to get a little angry to see how many drivers were ignoring the weather conditions and this particular vehicle had slid down an embankment. It was obvious that the driver had not respected or really paid attention to the conditions but as we drove closer to the heart of the scene our anger eased slightly as we watched our chief step out of the fire truck to assess the scene. He slipped on the ice, falling on his backside, sliding down the icy road, joining the car in the ditch. If not for one of our firefighters catching him, he would have ended up right underneath the ditched vehicle. We gave the driver the benefit of the doubt on this one.

The Pole Dance

When you think of a firefighter you might associate the following words: hero, fire hose, fire trucks, suspenders, uniforms and maybe even a fire pole. Did you think fire pole? Well, the pole is becoming a thing of the past and you won't see fire poles in newer fire halls as many injuries in the hall have been caused by sliding down them either incorrectly or too quickly. Many of the resulting injuries have been reported as twisted ankles and there are even instances where one has slid down the pole and landed on top of his colleague below neither of them realizing that the other was in the way.

Because of the injuries, the Workers Compensation Board has ordered them to be taken down and put out of service. This order came a little too late for one firefighter on a volunteer department who, in response to a fire call, went for a routine slide down the pole only on this hot summer day, he happened to be wearing shorts commando style (no underwear). Guys, you need to be sitting for this. You will never guess what happened next. When he slid down the pole, his shorts lifted and well, how can this be put nicely, he took his hose out of service by exposing his family jewels to the cool brass pole, breaking one of the jewels out of the treasure chest. In other words, he opened his fruit basket and used the pole to pull a grape off the vine. Either way, with a lot of pain and stitches, he is just fine now and has since stopped using the fire pole. He is now happy to use only the stairs to make it down to the lower level of the hall.

Mom, Can You Swim?

A non-emergency call was received by our fire department. It wasn't a typical rainy day as the whole past week had received record-breaking rainfall. When the call came in to our dispatch, the lady on the line told us her basement was totally flooded and her husband was at work with no one around who could help her deal with the lake that was quickly developing in her home.

We weren't able to help her as our department was not equipped for a situation such as this and the dispatcher instructed the lady to call a plumber. A short while later another call came in from the husband of the lady who had called earlier on. The man was quite upset that aid was not sent to his home when the original call was placed. He argued his case saying that not only did he pay taxes which went partially toward funding the hall but that his wife was six months pregnant and how could we deny her assistance.

Reluctantly we went to the house to keep peace between the patron and ourselves and to see if there was anything that we could actually do to help the woman in distress. Going into their totally flooded basement we found less than half an inch of water on the floor, definitely not the lake she had described. Even though the situation was not too serious, we still did not have the proper equipment to deal with the water and found ourselves using the neighbour's work shop vacuum to suck up the water.

Ahem…Excuse Me Please

Why is it that some people don't understand that the flashing lights and sirens on a fire truck mean GET OUT OF THE WAY? I have responded to calls where some of the other drivers on the road will just stop right in the middle of the road so now we have to come to a complete stop and wait for the opposite lane of traffic to clear before being able to proceed to the call.

One time there was a driver on a single lane road who, rather than pull over on to the shoulder, slowed down and continued to drive at a very slow pace along the road. No air horn, flashing lights or siren were going to get this driver to pull over out of the way…not even our hand gestures as we were forced to merge into the oncoming traffic to get around this vehicle. When we finally had the opportunity to pass, the driver gave us the rudest look, the kind that says 'who do you think you are?' 'Well we're the fire department, get off the road it's the LAW!!!'

Whatcha Gonna Do When WE Come For You!

When the alarm sounded, we were sent out to a medical aid call. The victim was unconscious due to a drug overdose. Our trucks approached the incident, with sirens blaring so loudly that the unconscious victim awoke and attempted to leave in a staggering fashion, not wanting to be arrested but by this point our chief's vehicle was blocking the driveway and not being fully aware, the victim rammed him out of the way with her car.

Well this isn't normally our job but the chief wasn't about to let this one get away, after all this was our patient and she had hit his car. The chase began and after not too long the victim drove her car directly into a ditch. Now she was definitely getting arrested as there was nowhere to flee.

Tantric Healing

A young man had the unfortunate luck of having heart problems at just 35 years of age. He had already had two heart attacks and suffered from angina. Like anyone would, he wanted to improve his condition so he decided to join a natural healing group. The group based their healing techniques on touch and spiritual thought. Naturally, in one of their sessions they put their tantric techniques to work and as they did so the man started having chest pains!

When the man's condition proved too much for their efforts they called 911. The fire department was first on scene and could not believe what they saw. The healing groups had the man lying on his stomach with his legs bent up into the air. As if the contortionism wasn't bad enough, all the members of the healing group placed their hands on him and were chanting which made his discomfort much worse. There was one believer of modern medicine in the group. This natural healer found the man's nitroglycerine spray and was spritzing it into the air in his general direction. Seeing his excruciating pain, without a moment of hesitation, we took over.

You Broke What?

Mechanical failure is bound to happen to everyone and yes, even the fire trucks will break down from time to time. This can be really embarrassing. There have been many instances of dropped drive shafts. Even though it's from general wear and tear, the driver always seems to get blamed and bugged about it. I heard that a newer firefighter had a drive shaft go, and his platoon captain told the rookie he needed to tell the chief and that he was really in for it! When he reluctantly made the trip into the chief's office to report it, the chief thanked him and told him that it was better now than if it had happened when they were on an emergency call.

Another firefighter using one of the department's smaller trucks for some duty work had no problems with the running of the vehicle. However, the next day when another crew member went to use the truck, it wouldn't start. When the mechanic had the motor half apart, he reported to the chief that the motor had seized up from driver abuse and that the truck needed a whole new motor. Well all fingers started to point and the firefighter pleaded that he had done nothing wrong. It didn't get settled until the mechanic's work order for the repairs came in and all it needed was a new starter and a tune up.

Doh!

So you know gasoline is flammable right? Well, one individual certainly seemed unaware of this scientific breakthrough when they proceeded to weld, not close to but actually on, a fuel tank. This caused a fire in his garage. Surprise, surprise.

His next scientific discovery was that spraying the fire with a garden hose actually spreads a gasoline fire. We arrived to a fully engulfed garage; we saved his house but couldn't do anything for his dignity.

CAT-apolt

People love calling the fire department when there little feline friends get stuck in trees. This kitty was stuck high up a very thin tree, unable to support a person's full weight; posing an interesting rescue situation. The firefighters opted to tie a rope as high as they could on the tree and use their truck winch to pull the tree down far enough to remove the frightened cat. The idea worked like a charm, they pulled on the tree, which was bending nicely, and the kitty was inches from their awaiting arms when the rope let go, shooting the cat VERY far through the air.

Stolen: One Fire Truck

The volunteer hall in this story was perched on top of a small hill. The department was called out to a bush fire and all but two of their resources were away from the hall. Two volunteers arrived at the fire hall, jumped into the ladder truck and radioed command that they would be responding to the call. Command replied that they required the rescue truck, as there had been some injuries. The two firefighters jumped out of the ladder truck and into the rescue truck and proceeded to respond to the scene.

Hours later all the fire apparatus returned to the fire hall, all except the ladder truck. First conclusions were that it had been stolen but upon further investigation, they found their ladder truck in the bushes inches away from the house that was across the street from the hall. The firefighter had forgotten to re-apply the parking break when switching trucks at the time of the call out.

I'll Handle This

Fire alarm bells sounded at an elementary school in the dead of the night. The duty chief was first to respond. After doing all the standard procedure searches, both in and out of the school, the duty chief determined that there was no fire and radioed the dispatch centre to let them know that it wasn't necessary for them to send assistance. The responding firefighters didn't think much of it until the next day when they saw the duty chief who now had a broken nose. He explained how he had slipped and fallen "and it wasn't a big deal...really things like this just happen."

The hospital accident report came back to the fire hall later that week and it was then revealed that the duty chief has actually been using bolt cutters to gain access to the school through a gate. He was using them improperly and when the lock broke, the bolt cutters came flying back into his face, breaking his nose.

Foot Loose

One of the problems a firefighter faces when responding to an incident in an unoccupied building is gaining access to the structure. First you must assess the situation and sometimes it is better to wait for the owner to show up, as no visible flames may be present.

When forced entry is required to enter a structure a window or door are the best methods of entry as they can be locked or secured upon leaving. One forced entry method that has been removed from firefighter training is to kick the door in. Not only does it not allow a controlled opening, which you need in a backdraft situation, you can also injure yourself. The biggest reason though for firefighters not to kick a door in, is because you look like a moron when only your foot goes through the door, leaving you dangling on the other side. This has happened many, many times.

Stop the Truck!!!

On every volunteer hall the members have jobs of their own and of course, lives and hobbies outside of the hall. One of our long time volunteers had an interesting hobby, taxidermy. For anyone not familiar with the term "taxidermy", it has nothing to do with taxes or taxicabs. Taxidermy is the art of stuffing dead animals. Whenever we were returning from emergency calls, this volunteer would have his eyes peeled, scanning the road for that "prized" road kill. If he saw something "good" he would try to convince us to stop, pick it up and put it in the fire truck. Much to his disappointment we always drove on by so he would have to come back in his own personal vehicle to collect his find. Just think of the cost he put into air fresheners for his car.

Don't Mess with the Instructor

Firefighters go through rigorous training to become qualified to do their jobs. One of the fun courses many take is an Emergency Vehicle Driving Course. While on this course, firefighters learn the limits of the trucks, gain backing skills and do a slalom course through cones in a full-sized fire truck with only inches on either side to spare.

Each morning before the actual driving takes place, the instructors will ask the students what they would like to learn on that particular day. There's always one or two hotshots who give remarks such as "I want to learn how to slide the truck out around corners," or "I want to learn how to put it on its roof." Once in the field, some of those hotshots would annihilate the cones in the slalom course.

The instructors always find their revenge though and send the broken cones back to the hotshot's fire department as a reward, a token of what their skills demonstrated. The cones come complete with their name and blunder written on them so that they will always remember their experience and, the instructor gets the last laugh.

Chief, Can I Have a Mohawk?

A department with many older firefighters had to start finding replacements for when they retire. Time and styles have changed and some of the older firefighters were against the wild hair colors, piercings and tattoos on some of the young recruits. One of them asked another senior firefighter why they kept bringing in all these 'young punks' and not older guys. The other replied because all their parts work. With that they revised the rules to state that no firefighter shall have a hair color, not naturally occurring in humans.

Donkey Doctor

A farmer had a non-emergency situation and did the right thing by not calling 911 and tying up the precious emergency lines. The farmer instead called the fire department directly, to see if they could lend a hand. The Chief picked up the phone and listened intently to the farmer's situation.

It turns out that one of his donkeys had fallen down a well. The Chief threw the farmer off when he asked if the donkey was having any breathing problems. Confused, the farmer replied…"Uh!? No….Why do you ask?" The Chief answered "I just wanted to know if we needed to send an ambulance as well." This particular Chief was known for having a good sense of humour.

Don't Mess with a Gorilla

A firefighter had met a new girl and was very excited at the thought of her; he couldn't get her out of his head. Valentine's Day was fast approaching and he thought that this was a perfect time to express his interest in her and to impress the socks off her. The firefighter worked the day shift at his hall on that Valentine's Day so he devised a plan - late into Valentine's eve, the firefighter armed with all the essential Valentine's Day token gifts: chocolates, roses, and the cutest Valentine's stuffed gorilla he could find (I'm not too sure why they make Valentine's gorillas but anyways...) arrived at her house to drop them on her doorstep. The love struck fireman stealthily snuck up to the unsuspecting girl's house dodging motion sensors and being as quiet as possible so that he did not wake the yappy little dog that slept inside the home.

He carefully placed the items on her doorstep along with a card bearing his special message of adoration and name. Feeling very confident he went off into the night.

The next morning on shift at the hall thoughts ran through his head - Did she get it? Will she like my gifts? Will she call here or will she call me at home after my shift? His racing thoughts were interrupted by a call out. The emergency scene turned out to be at the girl's home. As the crew drove up to the house, the fireman noticed that his offerings of love turned out to act more as obstacles than tokens of affection. The girl's father had awoken as he did every morning at the crack of dawn, left his house via the front door, to retrieve the daily paper. The only problem was that on this morning, he ended up tripping over a Valentine's Day gorilla injuring himself.

The firefighter was so embarrassed but luckily the girl's father wasn't hurt too badly and was in good spirits.

The fireman did get the girl so there was a happy ending...for two months at least, before they broke up!

Foam Party

A fire equipment supplier wanted to show off his new gear to some fire departments around the area. The equipment dealer had some of the local fire halls gather together at a large open field so that he could demonstrate his newest, greatest Compressed Air Foam System, also known as CAFS. CAFS like its' name states, use compressed air injected into the fire pump, increasing the volume of foam produced through the hoses. The foam then acts essentially as a 'wetting' agent for water. Foam makes water more effective at fighting fires by clinging to surfaces and lasting longer.

The equipment guys fired up their machines and went to work blanketing the field with foam. They were able to build a foam wall almost 15 feet into the air! The wall was so high that some of the firefighter groups couldn't see where other groups stood - it was a massive wall of foam!

Everyone was impressed, that is until the wind picked up. The gusts of wind grabbed a very large 10' by 10' ball of foam. The men then watched this ball sail onto the busy highway that was located next to the field. Luckily nobody was hurt when all the cars started locking up their breaks and performing other evasive maneuvers to avoid the giant bubble. Some drivers even ploughed right through it - beats the line up at the car wash huh?

Going Strapless

Part of a firefighter's job in a medical aid incident is to assist the paramedics getting the patient onto the stretcher or gurney.

A gentleman was in an automobile accident along with a few other people who had been riding in the same vehicle. Luckily the gentleman's injuries were not too serious but, to ere on the side of caution, the rescue crew put him in a neck collar and proceeded to load him onto a stretcher so that the paramedics could tend to him properly.

The paramedics loaded the gentleman into the awaiting ambulance and then went back to the scene to tend to the other injured victims. The firefighters were extracting another customer when they felt someone looking over their shoulders. The gentleman they had just removed from the involved vehicle was now peering over their shoulders to see if the other occupants were okay and wondered if he could lend a helping hand.

It seems that both the firefighters and the paramedics assumed that the others were going to strap the curious bandaged/collared individual down. Just goes to show that you should never assume anything.

Sweetie, Quit Flirting with my Friends!

Two backyard mechanics were out on their driveway 'tooling' around beneath one of their cars. The wife of one of the mechanics, the owner of the car, decided to go out shopping and before leaving she playfully grabbed, who she thought was her husband, in the groin as she said goodbye.

The trouble was that the man she grabbed wasn't her husband but his friend who, in shock, immediately sat up banging his head so hard on the car's undercarriage he knocked himself out cold.

Help was called and the unconscious man was placed on a gurney to be evaluated by the rescue team. The mechanic groggily awoke to find paramedics and firefighters all around him, which he found all too overwhelming, and in surprise fell off the gurney knocking himself out once again.

The Customer is Always Right

Two firefighters responded to a home where a Q-Tip was having difficulties breathing. Just to deviate a little, this department lovingly referred to elderly women with stark white hair, as Q-Tips.

Okay now back to the story...halfway to the hospital the Q-Tip asked if they could return to her home to fetch her fuzzy slippers because she couldn't go to the hospital and stay overnight without them, they were her favorite. To turn back to her home to retrieve the slippers would add an extra 45 minutes to their time on this call out, but they listened to the Q-Tip and backtracked to grant her request.

The family of the elderly Q-Tip was so impressed with the department's service that they called the Chief the next day to thank them for their kindness. The Chief called the crew into his office and asked them about their actions and how they had turned back for the slippers. The firefighters back peddled and tried to cover their butts, with faces crimson red. The Chief just smiled, he had actually brought the men into the office to congratulate them on a job well done. They had pleased and brought comfort to the elderly lady who was in a not so nice situation.

Who Ya Gonna Call?

True irony would be a fire hall burning down right? Well it has happened more than once, and who do you call when it does?

A fire hall had a mechanic shop in it that the firefighters were using to fix up one of their decommissioned classic trucks. The restoration project was going well and moving along quite quickly as all the men working on the project were putting in many late nights.

On this night they closed up shop and headed for home only to be called back several hours later to find their fire hall completely engulfed in flames. All that the fully trained firefighters could do was watch as the hall burned slowly to the ground as they waited for a neighbouring hall to respond. The cause of the blaze was determined to be from a hot ember smoldering from the welder they were using on their restoration project of their now completely destroyed classic truck.

911 Reports

Amazingly a lot of people don't understand that the "9-1-1" emergency service line is for emergency use ONLY!!! Some of the call-ins may be humorous but they may prevent an operator from receiving real emergency calls that could save someone's life.

Can you believe people will call 9-1-1 when they don't have a quarter for the pay phone and try to get the operator to call home for them, or when they are running late for work and ask "if you could just tell my boss something important happened…" Call-ins have even been about how to cook a turkey, sure that may be seen as an emergency to the person who is trying to prepare Thanksgiving dinner for the first time, but honestly, it is far from a life or death situation.

So maybe the solution is that they need to start teaching young children in school what can be classified and what shouldn't be seen as a real emergency. Below are excerpts from actual 9-1-1 calls received by dispatch centres:

Dispatcher: 9-1-1 what is your emergency?
Caller: I heard what sounded like gunshots coming from the brown house on the corner.
Dispatcher: Do you have an address?
Caller: No. I'm wearing a blouse and slacks, why?

Dispatcher: 9-1-1 what's the nature of your emergency?
Caller: My wife is pregnant and her contractions are only two minutes apart.
Dispatcher: Is this her first child?
Caller: No, you idiot! This is her husband!

*It has been asked on more than one occasion "what's the number for 9-1-1 again?"

*Did you hear about the woman who frantically called the fire department to report a fire in her neighbourhood? Well, when the dispatcher received her call he asked, "Can you please tell me how to get there?"

Very confused and flustered the lady replied, "Don't you still have those little red fire trucks?"

***We're going where?**

We were called out by the 911 dispatcher to a call involving a tongue twisting street name, the dispatcher just couldn't pronounce. After several attempts and many slurs and sputters she gave up and spelled out the street name, letter for letter.

***Something to Think About**
When the power goes out in the home, often the telephone line is still functional. The problem these days is that households are replacing all their telephones with cordless units, which don't work when

the power goes out. Even with the introduction of cell phones it would be a good idea to keep at least one corded phone in the house in case of emergency.

Red Light Means Whop!

A large city fire department was constantly changing shifts around on the crew. On this shift a petit female captain was put in charge of the crew. The firefighters secretly wondered how a little woman like that could possibly order them around.

Responding to a call, the big burley firefighter driving the truck found out exactly why he needed to listen to her. Arriving at an intersection, he slowed a bit and then drove through it, assuming that because his sirens and lights were engaged, any oncoming cars would stop for him. The policy of the captain's department was a little different and it was commonly known that the driver of the truck had to wait for everyone to be stopped before proceeding through the intersection.

Well the firefighter's slowing a bit then proceeding on through the intersection did not impress his captain one bit and she showed her dissatisfaction by walloping the driver across the face with her clipboard. She said "I don't want to die today thank you very much!" Not wanting to be her next victim, the firefighters never questioned her authority again and gave her as much respect as possible. She almost broke the firefighter's nose.

She is very very nice otherwise (just in case she reads this.)

Fear of Tight Spaces?

Chimneys, ventilation ducts and other tight spaces always make for some amusing stories.

Fire departments have had to cut criminals out of several tight spaces when the bad guys think they have beaten the system and get stuck in their getaway route. Our friends the police take over after we cut the nabbed criminal out just so they can be stuck in another confining space - a prison cell.

During the festive holiday season, chimneys pose another challenge for over-eager dads who dress up as Santa Claus. Yes, some of them do get stuck in the chimney when trying to make their child's dream of seeing Santa come down the chimney come true. We are then called to 'un-stick' them.

Some firefighters were called to a residence to remove a kitty that was caught in the home's chimney. The owner could not see the cat from the top or the bottom but could hear it meowing. The firefighters were forced to cut a hole in the chimney in an attempt to free the household pet. Unable to see the cat even after a few more holes had been made, they still heard the cat's whining. They decided to start feeling around the chimney shaft for the animal.

It turns out that the household cat was never really stuck in the chimney. As the firemen were trying to reach in for the rescue, the kitty ran through the living room. What they did find stuck up the chimney was indeed an animal. The entrapped customer was some sort of whiney frog that sounded like a cat in distress.

...Pants on Fire!

It was a very dry summer and because of the forest fire risks there was a "no open burning" ban in effect. We responded CODE 3 (lights and sirens) to a smoke sighting. Arriving at the scene we noticed a man doing yard clean-up work, but there was no smoke or fire to be seen. We observed the man diligently working in his yard as if we weren't even there. Keeping in mind we arrived in our 1,000 gallon pumper truck, lights flashing, sirens blaring and parked in his driveway. You would think that he might lift his head to acknowledge our presence wouldn't you.

As we exited our vehicle and walked toward the gardener, he apparently hadn't noticed the three of us because he went about trimming the dirt with a gas powered trimmer. Puzzled, I had to just about step on the trimmer before he looked at me and said,
"Can I help you?"
"Yes we're here about a smoke sighting that was reported. Do you know where this may be coming from?"
"I don't smell any smoke. Do you smell any smoke?" he smartly replied.
"We're just going to take a quick look around if you don't mind, sir." I politely answered.

During our search we only found dry cold charcoal from a long since burnt out fire but nothing else. The man was acting too strange; we could tell that something was up.

It was then that the Chief pulled up and again we interrupted the man from his yard clean-up. The man was now becoming irate and tried to get us to leave the premises, accusing us of trespassing. As firefighters, if we believe that life, safety or fire may be affecting an area we may enter without any kind of warrant or permission.

After some heated discussion the man admitted to smoking out a bee's nest. Meanwhile, the police were enroute as the man had broken the law because he could possibly do us harm in his agitated state. He tried to show the Chief where the supposed "bees nest" was but could not produce any evidence. The police officer who arrived on scene pulled the man aside and asked him what had happened.

"All I did was pour some chemicals on an ant's nest and it started smoking," was his response.

Because his story kept changing he did end up with a ticket for the incident. We can only make a guess as to what really happened to the burnt materials and we believe that the man extinguished them and hid them in his garage. The homeowner wouldn't have even been issued a ticket if he was straight up with us from the get go. Goes to show you that honesty is the best policy and it works out to be cheaper too.

Pass the Marshmallows

A Battalion Chief was out cabining with some friends in the winter. Since it was quite cold they needed to light a fire to heat up the icebox of a cabin they were staying at.

"Don't worry, I'm a fireman. I'll handle this" declared the Chief. Off he went to prove his talents and absolutely stuffed the fireplace with paper and wood so there would be no chance it would fail to ignite.

Sure enough the fire lit up with a roar, heating the cabin quite nicely. The only problem was that he had forgotten to open up the flue. The fire grew so big that flames were actually coming out of the joints in the chimney and the little cabin became engulfed with smoke.

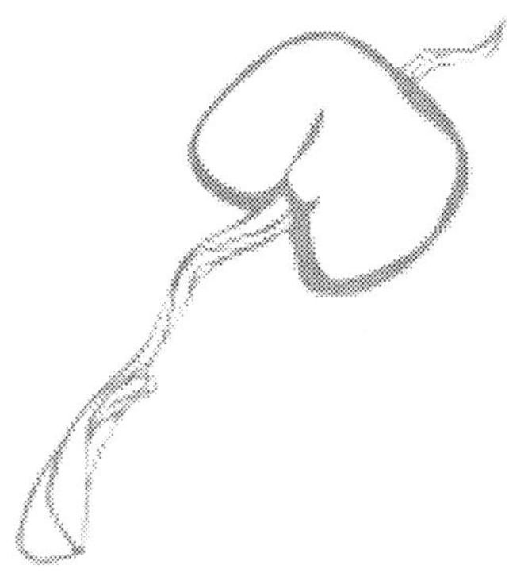

Um, Just Flip a Coin!

We rushed to an emergency call for an unconscious male in a vehicle. Since we were stationed in the rural community close to the victim, we were first to arrive on scene. The police and ambulance however did not have such a snappy response time as they had to come in from out of district.

The trouble with the call was that the road to which we were dispatched had the exact same name as a golf course in the district but the two weren't in the same vicinity, they were in opposing directions.

To make matters worse, the golf course named their private road after the course, the only difference between it and the other street was that the golf course added the word "Drive" to the street name and the other was called "Road".

The poor police officer was observed doing "U-turns" back and forth between these two roads. The ambulance however just drove past both of the roads all together and kept on going. Luckily, when we arrived on scene we found that the unconscious male was only taking a nap and needed no attention at all.

Attention: Firefighter Crossing!

Called to routine alarm bells at a local business, we arrived on scene to find that it was an actual fire and not a false alarm. We needed to immediately hook up to a hydrant which was a block away from the fire. The firefighter sent to do the task quickly grabbed the coupling on the first length of the hose and started to run full speed toward the hydrant.

When you pull hose off of the truck, with each consecutive length, it obviously increases in both weight and in the friction that has to be dragged, so stopping in mid pull is not really an option as you lose all momentum. As the fireman ran the hose, some traffic stood in the way of the hydrant. The firefighter was so determined to reach the hydrant without stopping that he ran straight for the traffic. Seeing this, the vehicles on the road knew that they had to make some evasive maneuvers and much like a Hollywood chase scene, they started swerving, backing up and doing anything else that they could possibly do to avoid hitting and getting in the way of the fireman and his hose.

Strange Occurrences

Called to an older stucco home for a possible fire under a window, we were surprised to find everything looking quite normal except for the odd small puff of smoke that was coming up from under a windowsill. We removed the drywall to further inspect the possible fire. To our astonishment the wood under the window was completely burned out! Puzzled we were unable to determine how this smoldering fire could have started. It was totally sealed inside the wall and there were no electrical wires close to this point. With the help of an electrician we found out what the problem was.

Apparently, a wire had been punctured at a totally different part of the house by a nail used to hold up the metal mesh for the stucco. For some reason, the electrically charged mesh was heating up another nail under the window which then caused the charring. This slow burning could have gone unnoticed for years, which is a scary thought!

Regular

The gentleman in this next story was a regular customer of our fire department. So much so that they no longer used his address on our pagers, instead they just paged us with his name and we knew exactly where to respond.

I guess you could say that he could be categorized as suicidal, but never really had any true intentions of killing himself. The man was a lonely, mentally ill person who just needed some attention. Many a call out we would respond to find him covered in blood from slitting his wrists again and again. If you looked around his place you would still see the dried blood stains from his previous attempts and our responses.

He was the one who always called 9-1-1 for himself. He had a severe dislike for the police, so whenever they needed information or wanted him do something, we would be called by the police to do their questioning for them.

He has since been moved to a home and has been trouble free for quite some time as he is now getting the attention that he both needed and deserved.

I Just Don't Like the Way It's Decorated!

The call came in over our pagers as a structure fire. It had been quiet lately and to have a call to respond to was exciting. Arriving on scene we found that only a trailer was involved and that a quick acting citizen had pulled a pile of burning newspapers out onto the ground and extinguished them in front of the trailer.

We inspected the scene and found that the fire had caused minimal damage and it was indeed extinguished. We were somewhat suspicious though as the trailer had been for sale for quite some time and the owner had left minutes prior to the fire.

We suspected that the trailer had been torched so that the owner could collect the insurance money. Not only did the owner do a bad job of trying to burn down his trailer, but as we were cleaning up, a couple interested in purchasing the trailer came to the scene.

Had it not had the fire damage they might have bought the amateur arsonists' unwanted liability.

A Real Monster!

Everyone knows one of those kids who just won't go to bed because it's dark, there's a monster under their bed, they hear noises outside, etc. and this next story begins as many spooky ones do...

It was a dark, stormy night and the family in this story had a child like the one described above. He just couldn't keep his head on the pillow and the thunder and lightning storm that was teaming outside his window wasn't helping the situation. After many attempts at putting the young boy to bed, the boy's father was getting tired of his son coming downstairs asking if he could sleep in his parents' bed. It was an innocent request as he was terrified to sleep alone that night. The father finally decided to let his son watch the television in his room in hopes that the child would be distracted by it, forget the eerie conditions outside, and doze off to sleep.

The boy came back downstairs once again.
"Just watch a bit of TV and everything will be alright son" said the father.

"I can't Dad" replied the boy.

Curiously the father sternly asked his son, "And why is that?"

His son's response was very simple, "It blew up!"

Rolling his eyes the father picked his son up and carried him back into his room, thinking that he should really consider investing in a lock for the bedroom door. As they entered the room, much to the father's surprise his son's television really had blown up and was smoking away.

Worried that there might be electrical problems the man decided it was best to call the fire department and fast - an electrical fire in the walls of the house was the last thing the man needed; plus it was always better to be safe than sorry.

When the fire department arrived and knocked on the door the man raced down the stairs to answer but before he could reach the bottom all that could be heard was his wife screeching at the top of her lungs:

"WAIT!!!! Whatever you do, DO NOT OPEN that door! You can't let them in yet."

The husband quite puzzled at his wife's request asked why and she abruptly answered,

"Because, I haven't got my makeup on yet!!!"

Can you just imagine the thoughts running through the man's head...

Upon inspection it was determined that the television was actually damaged by a direct lightning strike and there was a light tracing of the electrical arc on the wall behind the TV leading to the partially opened window. Luckily no one was hurt and there was no electrical fires running through the walls of the house. The only slight damage besides the young boy's television was his mother's ego - she had actually let a stranger see her without her face on. The horror!!

*Lightning is a very mysterious phenomenon and even scientists are not completely clear on how it is produced. One thing I know for sure is don't wash the dishes during a lightning storm. If you are in an older structure with metal piping and a metal sink you could quite possibly become the next victim of a lightning strike. One fire fighter found this out the hard way. He wasn't the direct path to the ground so he was only thrown from the sink and walked away from the hit virtually unharmed. The lightning had hit the fire hall's vent tube on the roof and traveled down through the pipes to the ground by the sink where he was standing. With his very valid 'lightning' excuse, his wife now has problems getting him to do the dishes.

Hall Mascot

There was a little Jack Russell terrier living across the road from our fire department. The dog was a curious little thing and would often watch us train. One day during a training exercise the little dog got too close and got soaking wet by our hose. From that day on, the dog was absolutely petrified of us and would dash away at the sight of us.

One of our guys was a bit of a character and told the rest of his shift buddies that by the end of the week he would have made nice with the terrier and that they would be friends. Each day this macho firefighter would get down on his hands and knees to attempt to coax the frightened pooch over to him. The dog would slowly inch toward him hunched down so low his belly dragged on the ground as his four little legs quivered away. By the end of the week it appeared as if the was going to let him finally get close enough to reach his hand out for a pet.

Then something changed, the dog was no longer timid and shy. As the fire fighter neared the dog with his outstretched arm the dog began to snarl, barring his teeth and bolted after the macho fireman. Startled, the fireman ran like his pants were on fire back to the station as the little monster ran close behind nipping at his heels. Narrowly escaping the terrier, the fireman decided it would be best for both of them to give up trying to be friends.

The Real Fire Hall Mascot

Today the Dalmatian serves as the hall mascot for the majority of fire departments. These dogs were an integral member of the force in the horse drawn fire cart days. Dalmatians and horses are quite compatible and the dogs could be easily trained to run in front of the horse drawn carts to aid in clearing a path and guiding the crews along their routes.

Dalmatians were first known as "coach dogs" and the record books report that their service dates as far back as the 17th century in England, Scotland and Wales. The dogs were used by well-to-do aristocrats who wished to stand out among their peers on the streets, running along side the carts. Because of their strong physical build, they are able to run for long distances next to or in front of the carts. The dogs also had a calming effect on the horses during exciting situations.

The dogs were not only seen as "man's best friend" but also horse's best friend. They were stable mates and would protect the horses from getting stolen in the night (horse theft by those less fortunate was very common in the olden days). They would also guard any luggage kept on board the coach from being looted during the evening.

There was a great deal of competition for services. Firefighters were recruited not only for their strength in fighting fires but also for their physical fighting abilities to protect the company and its equipment. Fire halls would earn their incomes from insurance companies who paid the first fire company that arrived on scene. The halls that had dogs would use them to quickly lead the fire carts through the busy streets which would speed up the response time of the crew. They could then quickly get hooked up to the hydrants and start pumping water on the blaze. The dogs performed well at both the leading task and protecting both the horses and the equipment from being stolen.

Dalmatians lost their role in the fire department when motorized cars and fire engines took over. Just as the old saying goes, "the dog is man's best friend" they are to this day still on duty in many fire stations, acting as companions to the firefighters and watch dogs of their equipment. They are seen as pets of honour by firemen as they symbolize heroism and strength.

Not Even for the Birds

A mutual aid call came out for a school on fire. Mutual aid is where a department has a situation too large to handle by itself and calls in bordering departments for help. This fire was very large and had flames shooting through the roof, up to fifty feet above the two storey school. There was no saving the school and our efforts turned into a defensive attack, which is also known as the "Surround and Drown" method.

One attack team thought that if they couldn't save the school, at least they could save the little bird house attached to a post at one end of the school. For several hours they were successful at keeping the little house unharmed from the blaze.

The attack team was eventually relieved from the call as the fire had been extinguished and the crews were now in a mop phase (cleaning up the scene). The birdhouse team packed up their things and got into their truck to return to the fire hall - their job was done. One last look where a once two storey school stood was now a pile of steaming rubble except for the birdhouse that still stood at one end of the pile. Sadly, as they drove away they looked back to see the little birdhouse had become consumed by the flames which was the only visible fire left. For the animal lovers, don't worry, the birdhouse was vacant and no birds were harmed in the fire.

Eager Beaver

A volunteer fire department had just bought a new ladder truck for their recently built fire hall. One of the eager guys on the squad jumped behind the wheel to drive it out of the apparatus bay. He forgot to account for the extra height of the ladder on the truck and drove out before the door had completely opened. Need I say more!!!

A Hair Raising Experience

A long-time firefighter and his wife were invited to a dinner party at a close friends' home. The evening was going very well and the two couples were sharing warm stories and laughs over drinks and appetizers, filling each other in on the happenings of their lives.

The couples sat down at the candle lit dinner table and passed around the food to begin their meal. As the firefighter's wife leaned over for the salad, her long blonde hair brushed against a candle and caught on fire! Luckily for some quick action, the flaming hair was extinguished, ironically though, not by her husband the professional fireman, but by his long-time friend.

Island Fire/Rescue/Detectives

When you run out of people to call, why not call the fire department. A customer on our Island's large ferry service from Vancouver Island to Vancouver jumped ship while enroute between the two ports. This was no accident. Apparently the fellow wanted to swim to one of the small Islands as the ferry made a near pass by. With a garbage bag inflated under each arm the patron proceeded to swim across to the Island.

The ferry sent out a rescue boat but the man wouldn't get in and just kept on swimming until he made it to shore. The small Island didn't have much of a police department so after eluding the police; the fire department was called to begin the manhunt.

Turns out that they did find the swimmer and upon questioning the truth surfaced as to why he abandoned ship. He was one of the locals from the Island who had missed his ferry but didn't want to wait for the next departure because if he had he would have missed his baseball game, so he jumped on the next available boat.

The last tidbit of news that was heard about this scenario was that the police were trying to charge him, but jumping off of a ferry is not a criminal offence.

What'd I Call You???

When the first leading firefighter arrives on the scene of an incident he establishes command over the radio and becomes the Incident Commander or I.C. for short. The I.C. is responsible for helping dispatchers and other responding units distinguish the scene from others. The name of a scene is usually a street address or a distinguishing feature of the building (i.e. the address, type of building, etc.)

There have been stories of one captain doing things a little differently. He would name the scene after something he would see when he arrived. His command calls would be things like little doggy, flowerpot, rusty car, and woman in slippers, etc. The other responding units would then have to address him by these names. So for example "Woman in slippers command…Engine 4 on scene, or Little Doggy command do you request assistance?"

To V Or Not to V? That is the Question

To ventilate a building you need to make an opening in an upper part of the structure which allows the super heated gases to escape. If ventilation is done too soon it allows oxygen to enter the building, feeding the fire and promoting flame spread.

Situation #1:

Two firefighters on top of a large commercial structure had the timing right for ventilation but not the location. With all the right power tools and equipment they were just about to go ahead and painstakingly cut through the very tough tar and gravel roof when another firefighter, not too far away yelled to the two, "Hold on." The firefighter walked over grabbed an axe and with one quick rap on the skylight directly beside the firefighters, successfully vented the roof with ease.

Situation #2:

A Captain was assessing a fire scene in an industrial building and wanted to determine the location of the fire before ventilation was done. If the wrong location is chosen the fire can be made worse. While doing his size up of the building, one eager firefighter went and smashed all the windows on one side of the building. Only trying to help, the firefighter inadvertently fed the fire with oxygen and the building ended up burning to the ground.

Bad Penmanship

We were called out to a possible assault with a stabbing and when responding to a call like this we always prepare for the worst. When we were close to the scene, we ran into an interesting obstacle - a very intoxicated female wandering back and forth across the road. After watching her for a few moments, she turned around and said in a slurred tone, "you'ze guys go ahead, you'll probably beat me there anyways." She then stepped aside for us to proceed to the call.

Now on scene, we entered the house to find more drunk people, one of whom was our stabbing victim. One of our firefighters grabbed the first responder form and began filling out the vital information about our victim. There was only one problem though; the pen she was using had run out of ink so she looked around for another and was handed one from a helpful drunken witness in the house.

The stabbing victim had apparently tried to take her own life and when one of the responders went to check the stab wound he couldn't find anything. The responder asked the intoxicated 'stabbing' victim, where she had stabbed herself. Our customer then pointed at her arm which had a dot on it. The dot was a pen mark; the woman had tried to kill herself with a pen and didn't do anymore damage than an ink spot before passing out from all the alcohol she had consumed that evening.

The responder then asked politely where the "weapon" was and the drunken woman pointed to the other responder. The firefighter had replaced the dried out pen with the evidence.

Have You Seen My Pet?

An off duty firefighter was on his way home from town to his countryside residence. He was sailing along the quiet country road when all of a sudden he had to come to a stop as he came upon a traffic jam; a strange occurrence for any country route. While waiting for the cars ahead of him to begin moving, he thought to himself, "why would there be such a tie up out here?"

He soon got his answer as a horse went charging by his car. The horse seemed to have a look of "ha, ha I'm free" on its face. Right behind the horse, only a few car lengths back, was the fire chief with his very best "why am I doing this?" face.

As the parade continued, a truck towing a horse trailer sped by, heading in the same direction as the fire chief and horse. The truck stopped to talk to some of the people who were stuck in the hold up. It was clear that they were looking for the horse when twenty or so people from a nearby wedding all pointed in the same direction towards the runaway horse.

Who Needs a Pulse Anyways?

On scene at a medical aid call we were responding to a gentleman with chest pains. The firefighter went to check the man's pulse and ran into a small problem - he wasn't wearing a watch and no clock was visible in the room to use to time the patient's heart pulses. Being resourceful, the firefighter got his helper to count out loud so he could get a somewhat accurate reading.

As the firefighter started to count out loud the patient thought that he would join in as well. The patient could not count at all. His count went something like this: "one, two, five, nine, etc." His pattern was totally random and he was even reciting things in the count that weren't even numbers. "Eight, dog, truck, eleven."

Well it turns out that the patient's counting was so distracting to the firefighter that he was not able to come up with a pulse rate. The strange part was the patient actually thought he was helping.

Want To Go For a Resuscitation Boy?

Now and again you hear a story about a firefighter saving an animal's life; you know a dog, cat, a horse, a pig and sometimes even weird animals like a lizard by giving it CPR (Cardio-Pulmonary Resuscitation). It sounds bizarre but how could you just sit there and tell a child that their favorite pet has died without even trying to do anything; oh the guilt that would be felt.

A neighbouring department decided that it would be best to take a proactive approach and purchased a rescue dog doll. This is a life size, realistic rubber dog (tongue and all) much like the human models and is used to practice CPR. I had no idea that something like this even existed. All of the surrounding departments thought this was the funniest thing ever and would call up and brag about having their own new rescue animals. They would joke about having rescue sheep, cats, squirrels, birds and even fish for CPR training at their departments. All I have to say, I hope they pick up after the CPR dog when they take it for walks?

Try That Red Thing the Dogs Pee On!

Rumor has it that there is a bumbling fire department out there that turned a routine, easily extinguishable fire into a smoldering foundation.

As the story goes, upon pulling up to the fire, they ran about, entered the building and started to knock the small blaze down and then ran out of water. They had forgotten to hook up their truck to the fire hydrant and by the time the matter had been resolved the fire was out of control.

To take action the crew were then seen throwing their pike poles, like spears towards the upper floors of the building. No one knows exactly why they were doing this, but it sure didn't follow the protocol of any department I have ever heard of.

Thrifty Recruit

A firefighter received some new station gear (the shirt and pants worn around a fire station on shift). Not wanting his still good and wearable old uniform to go to waste he donated the outfit to a local thrift shop.

This wasn't very thoughtful of him though. Within a couple of days one of the local street bums was out begging for change in his once neatly pressed fire department uniform that was complete with identifying shoulder patches. Not a good image for their fire department.

More Hazard, Less Duke

An old country road bridge had been removed and was being replaced with a culvert, which is more cost effective and has a longer lifespan. The construction certainly inconvenienced the locals because they had to use a detour route, adding about fifteen extra minutes to their drives to get in an out of the rural community.

One young guy, perhaps influenced by the new "Dukes of Hazard" movie, figured why waste time and use the detour when the ravine under the bridge wasn't that wide. So this 'Duke' decided to remove the barricade that blocked the road, to get a good run at the ditch and tried to jump it. As 'Duke' drove toward the jump he gained quite a lot of speed and as he approached the gully, the vehicle launched off of the pile of dirt, just like in the movies. UP, UP and...well, down he went only making it halfway across the ravine.

At this point the fire department was called to pull him out of his car that was lodged in the ditch. 'Duke' was very lucky he only came out with minor injuries to his face and body. Maybe next time he will get up a little more speed to make it 3/4's of the way across.

Send in the Clowns

A career hall was sent to a small grass fire and they were able to extinguish it in no time at all.

As the news crews showed up to report the incident, the firemen were in the midst of packing up. Seeing the opportunity to be in the spotlight, two of the more cocky firefighters on scene didn't want to let the news crews down (more like they wanted to be on T.V.) so they immediately sprang back into action! One of the hotshots yelled, "I found a hot spot" and started randomly spraying water. The other had a very large burned out log hoisted above his head "just moving it to a safer location" he grunted. Their platoon chief just stood and laughed at the two clowns.

Where's the Snooze Button!

When working a night shift, if there are no calls to respond to and all duties have been completed, a fire crew is generally at the hall catching up on lost sleep.

After being toned out, a big city fire department was second to arrive on scene late one night to a medical aid call. The paramedics had already arrived and one said to the fire Captain, "oh, sorry did the emergency call wake you?"

The fire Captain gave a disdainful look to the paramedic who he felt was mocking his crew for being second on scene. The Captain looked directly at the paramedic and said, "It's obvious that you don't need our help."

He then turned around and said to his crew "Let's go boys."

Following the orders of their Captain, the team left and the paramedics were left to deal with the medical call alone.

Clear!

In a First Response call to a chest pain complaint received for a woman we did everything by the book. The lady was conscious so there wasn't too much that we could do besides asking which medications she was on, if she had allergies, a history of the complaint, location and severity of the pain, etc... The reason why we ask all of this is so that when the ambulance arrives we are able to inform them on the situation and they then have an idea of what they are dealing with when shipping the patient off to the hospital for a more thorough check-up.

On a chest pain or heart related call out we bring our AED which stands for Automatic External Defibrillator. This is one of those machines you see in a hospital where they use the paddles on the chest and say "CLEAR" before an electric shock is administered to the heart.

Walking into the residence, a senior firefighter told one of the firemen to have the AED out of its case and ready to go. The firefighter pulled the AED out and set it beside the woman, just in case something was to happen. He then opened the lid so that the electrodes were also prepped. The problem was that with this particular model of AED it immediately starts talking when opened up and out of its case.

The first thing that it says is "place electrodes on patient's bare chest." The poor woman, who we were helping, looked so horrified after hearing this message. She thought we were going to rip her clothes off and start shocking her. The firefighter quickly closed the lid and muttered "OOPS" and then everyone continued doing what they had to.

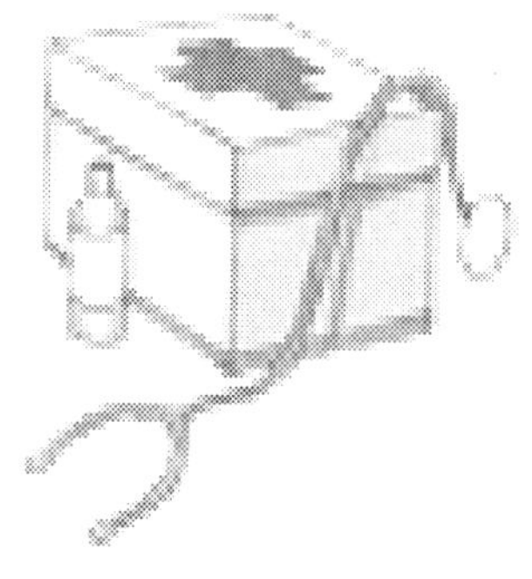

Ladies!

I would like to thank all of the ladies who have voted firefighting as the sexiest job. If it wasn't for these special women we wouldn't have cookies and other baked goods brought to our departments. Nor would we have regular "looky-loos" dressed up and made up at a scene like they're going on a date. We wouldn't have phone calls asking for single firemen to date. We always seem to make the lists for bachelorette parties.

Sometimes women flash us when we drive by in our trucks. We even get regular calls for kitchen fires that are easily controlled and the damsel in distress just happens to be dressed to kill even if she is oh, eighty or so. Hey, I've been in a firefighter bachelor auction for charity and saw first hand about four hundred women fighting to get some attention from the eight of us. The life of a fireman is great!

Okay, Who Took My Parking Spot?

Quick to respond to a call, a volunteer firefighter had completely forgotten the construction upgrades his department was involved in; because the community was growing, the department was putting a needed addition onto the fire hall.

The firefighter, in a rush to get parked and out of his car failed to observe the large hole that had been excavated for the new foundation. As he pulled up to the hall he absent mindedly drove towards his non-existent parking spot and his car went crashing into the middle of the large void.

Unharmed he managed to get out of his vehicle and climbed up out of the hole. He still made it onto a truck to respond to the call. That goes to show you the determination and devotion of our volunteers.

Rescue Me

On a self rescue training session at the fire house everyone was blind folded and sent through an obstacle course. The object was to simulate exiting a burning building with zero visibility while following your hose to safety. To make it difficult they added a rope entanglement section, obstacles to go over and under and at the end you were to breach a drywall panel and exit to safety outside.

It was our most keen firefighter's turn to do the drill. He always did every course and attended every practice but we all sensed that he lacked confidence only because he was afraid to make mistakes. Off he went, blind folded, into the course, following the entangled hose in the right direction through the ropes with text book skills, only while he was in the ropes, the other firefighters decided to play with him a little. They unhooked the hose he was following and rejoined it to itself making a large loop. So now our firefighter was going in circles as all the others giggled quietly. Once back at the rope maze the firefighter feared the worst; that he had screwed up! We let him think that for awhile before we told him what really took place. After a good laugh he wasn't afraid of messing up again.

I Need New Boots

Attention! general public if you see firefighters collecting money using a helmet, boot or anything else, no they are not collecting money for new boots! All of the fire departments in our local area help raise money for Muscular Dystrophy which is a rare neuromuscular degenerative disease primarily affecting the voluntary muscles. We call this charity fundraiser our annual "Boot Drive."

Each year the "Boot Drive" gets a little more exposure and word has really spread around that firefighters are volunteering to collect money for a good cause. The reason I bring this up is that because every year we get comments such as "there's nothing wrong with your boots," or "you already get paid enough through my taxes," "why don't you work like the rest of us," "I only donate to those in need." If you see us out there at least smile, the money is not for us at all.

Sea Monster

It is an urban legend that has gone around for while but, like many legends, no one really knows if it actually took place. The possible and believable story goes like this:

Firefighters were at a marina, busy trying to extinguish a blaze on a moored yacht. One of the firemen lost his balance and fell into the water and with his heavy fire gear on immediately sank to the bottom of the harbour. Since it wasn't too deep the Self Contained Breathing Apparatus (SCBA) he wore was still able to function. The other firemen simply watched as he walked along the sea floor to the boat ramp and then up to safety. Draped with some strands of seaweed, he was completely unharmed in any way, just a little wet and cold.

A curious fire department hearing about this possible story later contacted the SCBA company to verify if it were at all possible for a person to breathe underwater while wearing an SCBA. They would only speculate that their devices would function properly in up to 20 feet of water.

Trick or Treat

Hallowe'en is always a big event at our fire house. We invite the public in for hotdogs and hot chocolate. There is a huge bonfire which is followed by a fire works display. The community shows up to our event dressed in their best costumes and carve the most interesting pumpkins to be judged in the pumpkin carving and costume contests.

This year was no different and everything was going smoothly. Our bonfire was lit and was being carefully watched by some of our guys. Just as we began to relax and enjoy ourselves the tones went off and we were sent to an address near our hall for reported trees on fire. All the firefighters jumped on the trucks and we went en route to the fire, keeping our eyes peeled for suspicious looking teenagers in the area who may have caused the blaze.

We did not see anyone suspicious nor could we find the fire. When we turned around we found that we had been called out by a concerned citizen to our own bonfire. We got so carried away and the fire was so huge that it looked like a small forest fire from a distance. We don't make them quite that big anymore.

Embarrassing Moments With Your Hose

*If you're too rough on the clutch, especially on a hill, you can lose all of the neatly folded hose off of the back of the truck. The only option if this happens is to pull over and reload the deck with the hose while everyone looks and drives by.

*Attack lines are often folded neatly on top of the truck, ready to go. When the attack team is put into action they grab a line then call for water. Sometimes the pump operator can get confused which hose they have grabbed and charge the wrong one. The result is that the once neatly folded lines on the engine now resemble an exploding accordion; as the hose fills with water it flip flops everywhere.

Did You Know…

*Have you ever noticed older fire departments have spiral staircases? The reason for this is that when horse drawn carriages were being used, the horse was used to tow fire pumps. In the hall, the horses were left on the main floor (similar to where today's trucks are kept, on the main floor of the bay) and at that time the staircases in the halls were nice and straight. Horses being somewhat intelligent animals figured out how to climb the stairs and make their presence known on the upper level of the hall. Someone then came up with the bright idea to make the staircases circular so the two forces in the department couldn't mix. The horses never did figure out how to use the fire poles though.

*A high percentage of all firemen reportedly have pyro tendencies. Fitting isn't it!

*Some fire truck pumps draw so much water that they can cause cavitations or implosions in water pipes and even hot water tanks.

*A standard 50' length of $1^{1/2}$" hose weighs around 52 lbs and carries approximately 5 gallons of water when fully charged (when the hose is completely full of water). This means that the standard $2^{1/2}$" attack line with four 50' lengths can weigh around 400 lbs and you thought the hardest part of the fire service was carrying the people.

*In forest fires there is a funnel attachment for the fire hose which is used to catch water from streams or rivers uphill from the fire. What good would that do, you might ask? Well here is a formula to ponder: With gravity, water in a hose gains half a pound per square inch (PSI) per foot. So if you had too many hoses joined together you could end up with unsafe pressures. For example 600 feet of hose would have 300 PSI at the nozzle.

*Fire needs three basic components to survive. If you remove at least one of them the fire cannot sustain itself. The three parts are heat, fuel and oxygen or oxidizer.

*Fires today burn much hotter because of the synthetic materials used in new structures and furnishings.

*Although steel is not flammable it can be more dangerous in the case of a heavy fire load. A 50' or 15m steel beam heated to 1000^{0}F or 538^{0}C can elongate up to 4" or 100mm it also twists and buckles which can cause walls to be pushed outwards and collapse. If a steel beam is heated to 1200^{0}F (which is not at all uncommon for a modern structure fire to reach) the steel beam can no longer support its own weight.

*Have you ever heard the term 'water hammer'? Well 'water hammer' is the knock or ping sound that you hear when water is being shut off to quickly. The sudden stop of the flow of a water stream in the system is what causes the noise. 'Water hammer' is quite powerful having the potential to destroy fire pumps, burst hose lines, ruin fire hydrants, and even can cause main water pipes to explode!

Fire Funnies

Smarter Than You

There was a pilot and three passengers (two firefighters and a genius) on a plane when the plane's engines let go. The pilot came back from the cockpit wearing a parachute and said,

"Sorry guys I'm the pilot, this is my plane therefore I get one of the three parachutes on board."

The pilot jumps out of the plane leaving the three passengers alone to figure out who gets what safety device. Without hesitation the genius exclaims,

"I am one of the smartest men in the world and the world needs me."

Without even a pause he grabbed a parachute and jumped out of the plane. The older firefighter then turned to the younger one and said,

"Listen kid, you take the parachute. I've had a good life and you have so much ahead of you to look forward to."

The young fireman smiled and was very thankful for the sacrifice, he replied,

"No need to worry sir, the genius grabbed my backpack not the parachute."

Brown Baggin' It

There were three firefighters fighting a severe fire in the downtown core of their large urban city. This particular fire was so large that it spanned several city blocks. It took many man hours and crews to get the blaze under control. The three firefighters in this story were getting ready to sit down to have a much-deserved lunch break even though the fire was still roaring away.

As the two firefighters and the lieutenant sat down and opened their lunch boxes, all three discovered that their wives had packed them the same sandwich, peanut butter on whole wheat bread with the crusts cut off. The men then agreed that if they all shared the same lunch again the next day that they would jump into the flames together.

The next day, the three met again and when they opened their lunches to compare meals they discovered that they all had identical lunches again. So keeping to their pact, they jumped into the fire and died.

A joint funeral was held for the three firemen. The reverend asked the first firefighter's wife:

"Why are you crying?"

The first firefighter's wife said "Well I fixed him a lunch that I knew he didn't like but if he had only told me what he had wanted I would have made that for him."

The reverend then went on to ask the second firefighter's wife and her response was the same as the first wife. While the other wives were in tears the lieutenant's wife was laughing hysterically. When the reverend asked:

"What are you laughing about?"

"That idiot packed his own lunch every day!!" responded the lieutenant's wife.

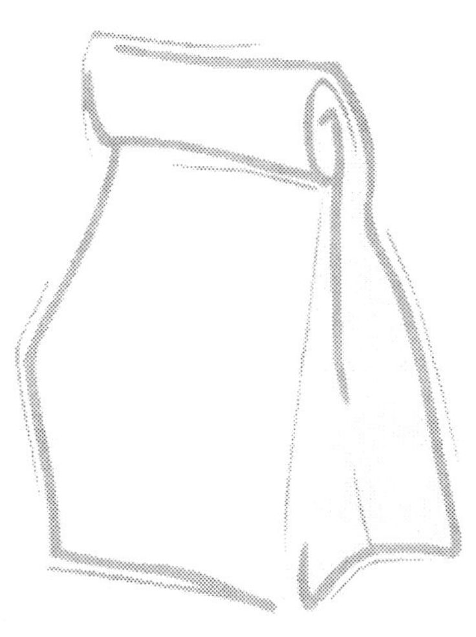

Stranded

Three blondes were stuck on an island. A little fairy appeared and asked the first blonde, "If you had just one wish, what would it be?" The blonde said, "I wish that I was smart."

POOF! The blonde's hair was instantly turned black and she swam off the island.

The fairy went over to the second blonde and asked, "If you had just one wish, what would it be?" The second blonde responded, "I wish that I was smarter than the other blonde."

POOF! Her hair turned brunette and she built a ship and sailed off the island.

The fairy then went to the last blonde and asked one more time, "If you had just one wish, what would it be?" The third blonde said, "I wish I was smarter than the other two blondes."

POOF! The blonde was turned into a firefighter and she walked across the bridge.

Peg Leg

A security guard with two wooden legs was on duty one night when the factory he was watching caught fire. The fire brigade saved the security guard but the factory was burned to the ground. To make things worse he was then arrested for arson...the judge said he was guilty, and he didn't have a leg to stand on.

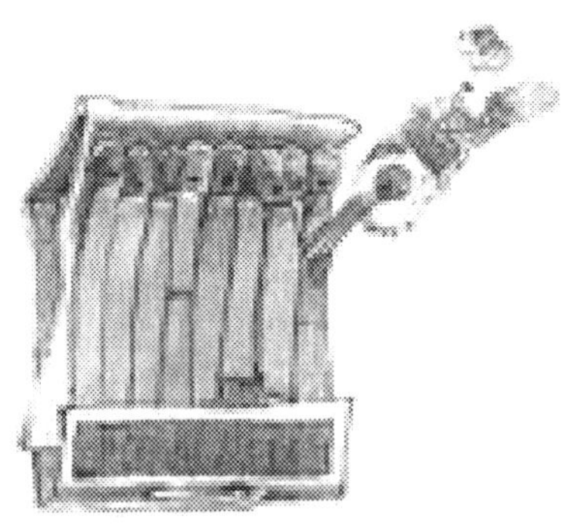

Just Call the Volunteers

A fire started on some grassland near a farm and the county fire department was called to put out the fire. When the fire department arrived they quickly became aware that the fire was more than their small crew to handle. One of the firemen suggested that they should call in a nearby volunteer hall for help. Despite some resistance and doubt that the career men had in the capabilities of the volunteer guys, the call was placed.

The volunteers arrived in a dilapidated old fire truck, rumbling straight into the fire before coming to a stop! The volunteer firemen jumped out and frantically sprayed water in all directions. Surprisingly, it didn't take them long to snuff out the middle of the fire which broke it into two easily controlled fires.

Watching all of this, the farmer was so impressed with the volunteer bunch and so grateful that they saved his land, he handed them a cheque right there on the spot for $1000. A local reporter asked the fire chief what he was going to do with the money. The chief responded, "That oughta be obvious. The first thing we're gonna do is fix the brakes on our fire truck!"

Skydiving

Did you hear about the fire that broke out last week in the six-story apartment building? A blonde, a redhead and a brunette narrowly escaped the flames by climbing up onto the roof. When the fire department arrived they got out a blanket and held it up while the fire chief called out to the women on the roof to jump into the blanket.

The brunette went first and as she was falling the firefighters pulled the blanket away and she landed on the street like a brick. The firefighters then held the blanket back up and the chief called up to the redhead and asked her to jump.

"No Way!!! I saw what you did to my friend!" exclaimed the redhead.

"I'm sorry," said the chief. "My wife was a brunette and she divorced me. I just don't like brunettes. We have no problems with redheads. Jump, it's your only chance."

After pausing for a moment to think about what the chief had said the redhead decided to jump. On the way down the firefighters pulled the blanket away again and the redhead hit the pavement like a tomato!

The firefighters again held up the blanket and the chief called up to the blonde, asking her to jump.

"No. I am not jumping. I saw what you did to my two friends."

The chief apologized once more "I'm sorry. I explained what happened to the brunette and well, when the redhead jumped we were distracted. It will not happen again, just jump!"

The blonde thought for a moment. "Okay, I'll jump but first I want you to lay the blanket on the ground and back away before I jump into it."

How firefighters identify a HAZMAT chemical using the Tri-COP-Scope Method:

1. Officer standing/car running - Not hazardous
2. Officer unconscious/car running - Toxic fumes
3. Officer unconscious/car stalled - Oxygen displacing chemical
4. Officer/car both melting - Acidic chemical
5. Officer/car on fire - Extremely flammable

Kids Say The Darndest Things

For Christmas a little boy got a bright red toy fire engine and it was his favourite present. A few days after Christmas, while playing with his new prized fire engine the little boy's mother listened to him from the kitchen and was shocked to hear what her son was saying. He was acting like the old captain rolling up on a structure fire:

"ALL RIGHT GUYS, GET YOUR %$#@ TOGETHER AND PUT THAT &^%#@ FIRE OUT NOW!!!"

Just beside herself at the language coming out of her son's mouth, she ran into the room where he was playing and scolded him, sending him to his room for a two hour punishment.

Two hours later the young boy came out of his room and went back to playing with his fire engine.

"ALL RIGHT GUYS LET'S MOP IT UP." Resuming his role as the fire captain, he turned to the imaginary owner of the house and said, "If your *&$@!% about the two hour delay, talk to the old bat in the kitchen"

Spot. What's He For?

A young mother was taking her turn with the community car pool, driving her minivan full of young kids home from kindergarten when a fire truck with its lights flashing flew past them and the siren at full blast. Sitting in the front seat next to the driver of the fire engine was a Dalmatian. The children, never having seen a dog in a fire engine before, got really excited and started to talk about what the dog might be for.

"They use him to keep crowds back," said one youngster.

"No," said another, "he's just for good luck."

Several more ideas were put forth by the kids and an animated discussion ensued. Then one of the little girls who had been sitting quietly through the discussion finally broke her silence, bringing the argument to a close...

"They use the dog," she said firmly, "to find the fire hydrant."

Fire Truck

A fireman was working on the engine outside the station when he noticed a little girl next door in a little red wagon with little ladders hung from the side and a garden hose tightly coiled in the middle.

The young girl was fully dressed as a firefighter. She had the wagon tied to a dog and a cat. The firefighter walked over to her to take a closer look.

"That sure is a nice fire truck," the firefighter said with admiration.

"Thanks," replied the little girl.

The firefighter looked a bit closer and noticed that she had tied the wagon to the dog's collar and to the cat's tail.

Slightly confused the firefighter asked,

"Little partner, I don't want to tell you how to run your fire truck, but if you were to tie that rope around the cat's collar, I think that you might go faster."

The young girl responded, "You're probably right, but then I wouldn't have a siren."

Bikers

There were these two guys driving a motorcycle down a dusty country road. The guy who was driving was wearing a leather coat that didn't have a zipper or any buttons, so the flaps of the jacket were flying in the wind.

Finally, the driver stopped the bike and told the other guy, "I can't drive anymore with the cold air hitting me in my chest." Inventive as he was, the guy decided to put his jacket on backwards to block the air from hitting him.

That problem solved, again the two men sped off down the country road. As they approached a sharp bend in the road the bike skidded out and they crashed in front of a farm.

The farmer that lived there called 9-1-1 to report the accident. When the fire department arrived on scene they asked the farmer "are either men showing any signs of life?"

The farmer replied, "Well, that first one was 'til I turned his head around the right way."

Clock Speed

A firefighter died and went to hell where he found a wall of clocks.

After seeing all the clocks on the wall of hell with his friends' names under them, he asked the devil, what was the significance of the clocks.

"That's easy," replied the devil, "each time one of your friends messes up on earth, their clock speeds up by one hour."

"Why doesn't the chief have a clock on the wall?" asked the fireman.

The devil looked at the fireman and responded "Well we decided that it would be best to put his down in the basement...... we're using it for a fan."

You Know that You're A Member Of A Redneck Volunteer Fire Hall If...

*Your department has had two emergency vehicles pulled over for a drag race on the way to a call.

*You have naked lady mud flaps on your pumper.

*You've ever come back from a call and found out that you locked yourselves out of the firehouse.

*Fire training consists of everyone standing around a bonfire getting drunk.

*You've responded to an outhouse fire.

*That outhouse fire was with entrapment.

*You've ever let a person's house burn down because they wouldn't let you hunt on their property.

*At least one vehicle in the fire hall still has decorations on it from the Christmas Parade and it's April.

*Your personal vehicle has more lights on it than your house has in it.

*You don't own a Dalmatian, but you do have a coon dog named Sparky.

*You've ever walked through a Christmas display and you come up with more than 3 new ideas for a light scheme for your truck.

*Your rescue truck can smoke its tires.

*Your department's name is misspelled on the equipment.

*Your engine had to be towed in the last Christmas Parade.

*Dispatch can't mention your name without laughing.

*The local news crew won't put your department on TV because you embarrassed them last time.

*You've ever referred to a light bar as sexy.

*Your defibrillator consists of a pair of jumper cables, a marine battery and a fish finder.

*You've ever taken a girl on a date in a pumper.

*Your pumper has been on fire more times than it has been to a fire.

*Your pumper smokes more than the house fire.

*The only time the trucks leave the station is on bingo night.

Pin Puller

When the employees of a restaurant attended a fire safety seminar, they watched a fire official demonstrate the proper way to operate a fire extinguisher, something very important to know how to do in a busy kitchen.

"Just pull the pin like you would pull the pin out of a hand grenade," explained the official, "then press the trigger to release the foam."

An employee was chosen to extinguish a controlled fire that had been built in the parking lot. In her nervous state the employee forgot to pull the pin.

The instructor, shaking his head, made the suggestion "Like a hand grenade, remember?"

In a burst of confidence she pulled the pin - and hurled the extinguisher at the blaze.

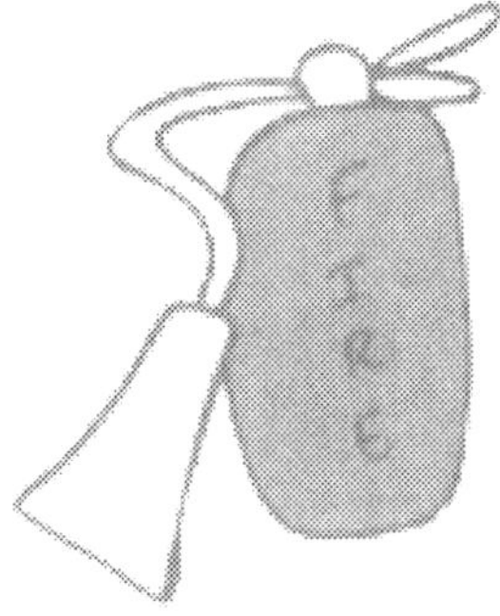

Pregnant?

Mrs. Thompson, a fourth grade teacher asked her students one day,

"Class, can you please write down a sentence which describes the work of a public servant?"

When the students were done, Mrs. Thompson asked each student to read their sentence out to the entire class. When Jimmy's turn came he read, "The fireman came down the ladder pregnant." Quite puzzled the teacher asked "Do you know what it means to be pregnant Jimmy?" Jimmy responded confidently, "Sure I do. It means carrying a child."

Respecting Officers

A lieutenant wanted a treat from the vending machine at the hall but didn't have any change.

Looking around to see if there was anyone nearby who looked like they had extra coinage, he spotted firefighter Elroy, a new recruit on their squad, mopping the floors of the bay.

The lieutenant asked "hey rookie, do you have change for a five?"

Elroy replied, "Sure."

The lieutenant gave him an icy stare as he didn't really like the tone in Elroy's response. He said, "That's no way to address a superior officer! Now let's try it again. Firefighter do you have change for a five?"

The young crew member replied with authority, "NO SIR!" and continued mopping.

Packed Plane!

Breaking news: There is a report that a two-seater, private plane has crashed into a cemetery. The fire department has reported recovering over 300 bodies and they're still digging.

The Real Meaning of Prayer

A preacher and a fire chief are on the steps of the Pearly Gates awaiting entrance by Saint Peter. The fire chief immediately passes through with out any questions. The preacher on the other hand met with resistance.

The preacher shocked at his refusal began stating to his superior that he knew for a fact that the fire chief was a totally sacrilegious man, a real trouble maker and a discredit to the human race as opposed to himself who lived an honest life, preaching the Word of God, saving souls, and cared for his fellow man.

Saint Peter responded to the preacher, "My dear man, your case has to be examined more fully. We have to look a little deeper to who we let in past the Pearly Gates to Heaven. After all, during many years you did preach the Word of God from your pulpit however many of those in your congregation would fall asleep during your sermons. While the chief drove his fire engine everyone would pray!"

Is Your Daddy Home?

In a desperate state, the boss of a big printing company needed to call one of his employees at home about an urgent problem with one of the computers in the office. The boss dialed his employee's home number and after a few rings a child's voice answered softly, "Hello?"

In a rush and taken aback by the child answering the call the boss asked, "Is your Daddy home?"
"Yes he is," whispered the child.
"Well, may I speak with him then?" To the boss's surprise the small voice answered, "No you may not."

The boss just HAD to speak with his employee so he asked the child again, "Okay well then is your Mommy there?"
"Yes she is," was the child's response.
"Well then can I speak with her?"
Again the quiet voice whispered, "No you may not."

The child sounded very young and the boss knew that it was not very likely that he would be left home alone, so the boss decided to leave a message with the person minding the child. "Is there anyone there besides you, little guy?" asked the boss.
"Yes," whispered the child, "a policeman is here."

Wondering what a police officer would be doing at his employee's home, the boss asked the child, "May I speak with the policeman please?"

"No, he's busy." whispered the child.
"Busy doing what?" asked the boss.
"He's talking with Daddy and Mommy and the fireman."

Now the boss was becoming a bit concerned and slightly worried as he heard what sounded like a helicopter through the ear piece of the phone. He asked the child, "What is that noise?"
"It's a hello-copter," answered the small voice.
"Well why is a helicopter flying overhead?" asked the boss with an alarmed tone to his voice.
In a quiet whispering voice the child responded, "The search team just landed the hello-copter!"
Alarmed, concerned and more than just a little frustrated the boss asked, "Why are they there?"
Still whispering, the young child replied along with a muffled giggle, "They're looking for me!"

Q & A's

Q: Have you ever wondered why it is so expensive to fight a fire in lower Manhattan?
A: They use bottled water!

Q: How do you tell which locker belongs to the female firefighter at the hall?
A: Easy, her locker is the one with at least twenty pairs of boots below it.

Q: What do firefighters and the police have in common?
A: They both want to be firefighters!

Q: Why doesn't a fire chief look out the window in the morning?
A: Because he wouldn't have anything to do in the afternoon.

Q: How do you put out a fire?
A: Take away the HEAT, FUEL, OXYGEN, or the CHIEF!

Q: Why do firemen wear "red" suspenders?
A: To hold up their pants. Duh.

Q: Have you ever wondered how many firemen it takes to change a light bulb?
A: Four; one to change the bulb and three to chop a hole in the roof.

Q: If H 2 0 is on the inside of the fire hydrant, what is on the outside?
A: K 9 P

Q: What does CHAOS stand for?
A: The Chief Has Arrived On Scene.

Q: What is the first thing off the fire engine at a trailer fire?
A: A lawn chair.

Q: What do you do if you see a fireman?
A: Put it out man!!!

Pranks and Gags

In any fire house you will see pranks played on many new recruits, regular firefighters and sometimes even the odd gag is played on the Chief himself. Now these pranks are often harmless but at times they can sadly get out of hand. Unfortunately because many of these pranks 'cross the line' they are often frowned upon but I've decided to tell you about them anyways...

On any career hall, during night shift after all duties are finished and there are no calls to attend to the firefighters are allowed to sleep at the hall - this keeps them rested and ready to spring into action when the tones go off. To be able to sleep you obviously need a bed, right? But with a bed comes the classic 'short sheeting' which is when the target firefighter's bedding is folded in such a way that they can only get in about halfway.

Besides short sheeting you will also hear about firefighters placing strange things into the bed sheets of their colleagues, like snakes, cracker crumbs, bugs, etc...

If the department has bunk beds then a whole new can of worms is opened. You might see someone come crashing through to the bunk below because his co-workers have removed the pins that hold the mattress up.

One new recruit was sent to the store to get some ice cream and when he got back to the hall he found his bed, alarm clock, night stand (the entire contents of his room) had been moved into the men's washroom. He was left with quite a dilemma. He asked himself, "Now do I sleep here in the bathroom or move my stuff back?" What would you do?

One group of pranksters had very dark sleeping quarters so they decided that while the newest recruit was in a deep slumber they would move his bed around so it faced the other way. When the alarms sounded the recruit in the backwards bed jumped up and still a bit disoriented in the darkness ran right into the wall.

If they can get away with it some firefighters have tried putting concentrated baby powder into the sheets of their partners' beds and then watched the ghostly looking individual run for his gear when responding to a call.

Another harmless but safe prank is to place empty pop cans under the legs of the bed. When the unsuspecting victim jumps into it, the cans crush so loudly that they think they've broken the bed.

If you really want to get one of the guys on your hall, try this out. When he gets up to go the bathroom in the middle of the night, have the toilet covered with clear, plastic wrap so tightly that it can't be seen. Just be prepared to run.

One large city fire platoon was sneaking glass, vial stink bombs into other fire platoons apparatus so when they got back into their trucks after a call, the stashed vials would break open and the crew would be forced to open their windows to air out the stench.

A really mean prank to play on your pals is to turn their boots backwards in their bunker pants so when the calls come in the firefighter doesn't have time to change them around and goes to the scene with his pants on backwards.

Another source of fire hall amusement is to change around the recruits' gear on their hooks so large built guys are forced to try to squeeze themselves into a smaller guys gear when a fake call is sounded.

On a night shift if you feel like getting in touch with your domestic side and you can get a hold of one of your comrade's pants try hemming them so much so when he puts them on for the next call he will be sporting trendy flood pants.

Boots are also easy targets that make great containers for water, drink crystals (for changing foot colours), itching powder, and anything else you could think of to put in them.

A really popular hazing prank to play on someone at a forestry practice. Part of the forestry practice involves filling portable tanks also known as pumpkin tanks with water for the purpose of drafting from the trucks. These large tanks are perfect for throwing the new recruits into.

To practice first aid part of the training involves handling spinal injuries. To practice these techniques the recruit is asked to lie on the spine board and then another fireman shows the other,s in the training session how to properly strap down the victim. When the recruit is firmly strapped down a fake call is placed to the hall and all the crew pretends to respond, leaving the recruit attached to the board.

How do you get one of your 'old boys' who has seen it all? Well at the next retirement party I dare you to try this next prank. Get a picture taken of the old guy in front of one of the fire trucks. Then hide one of your men above the retiree on the truck, so when the picture is snapped the guy above the lets a bucket of icy cold water fly.

How would you feel as a new recruit if all your new co-workers were only wearing boxer shorts and boots as they went about their day?

One prankster got a taste of his own medicine when the other firefighters decided to get together and tied a box with a few pop cans in it (just enough to weigh the box down) to his bumper. They wrote "Free Kittens!" on the box and as the guy drove down the road, unknowingly dragging the "Free Kittens!" box he couldn't help but noticing that tons of people were yelling at him. He finally found out why he was being snarled at when an angry police officer pulled him over to point out his bumper attachment. Everything was eventually smoothed over once the box was removed from the bumper and it was revealed as just a gag.

A brand of Self, Contained Breathing Apparatus (SCBA) has a hose that runs off of the face mask so when worn and not breathing from the air tank the firefighter will look like an elephant with a trunk. This leaves you wide open to being taken advantage of. Firefighters would then grab at the air supply hose of fellow men on their platoons and holding the hose near their rear, ridding their pent up gas. Breathing is one of those essential things we all gotta do, so you can only imagine what kind of torture this would be.

Many departments have banned pranks so one fire hall got their recruits to haze themselves. They would do this by placing a bucket in the middle of a room, the bucket was full of water and had a note attached that read, "Dump water on head." Would you believe that some recruits would actually do this?

REJECTED MISSION STATEMENTS AND SLOGANS

- You light em' we fight em'
- Has your family been touched by our fire department?
- We do our best and if you have insurance it will cover the rest.
- Who ya gonna call?
- We treat your stuff like it's our own
- In our department's history we've never lost a single foundation
- Show us your fire and we'll show you our hoses
- We're known for more than just our poles
- Dial 911 for a date with us.
- Still the best water delivery service.
- Come on baby light my fire.

Conclusion

So you managed to get through the book!!! Well if I made you laugh then I have achieved by goal. If you didn't crack one smile, not even once then I hope maybe you learned something new.

These are my final words that I will leave you with:

Dare to dream and learn to meet your goals! Before this book I wasn't too sure if I was even literate let alone capable of producing a book.

Thank you for taking the time to read my words.

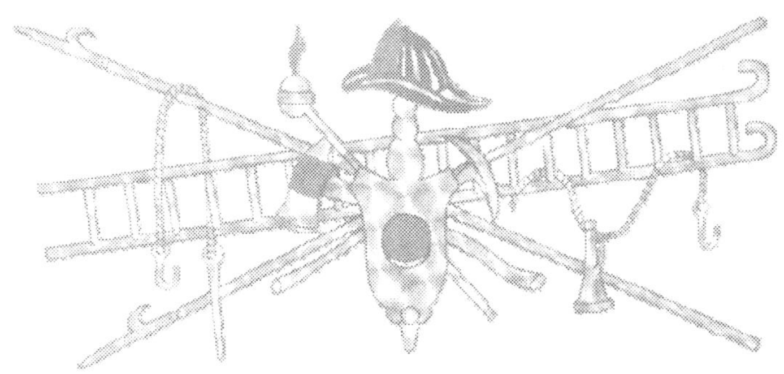

Contact Information

To reach the author, Ben Hughes, with any questions, comments or to share firefighting stories you would like to see published in the future, please send an email to:

thelightersideoffirefighting@hotmail.com

Cover Photography by Genevieve Primeau

Email: odinis@shaw.ca

Printed in the United States
133277LV00001B/211/A

9 781412 071710